Chapter One
Chapter Two
Chapter Three
Chapter Four
Chapter Five
Chapter Six
Chapter Seven
Chapter Eight
Chapter Nine
Chapter Ten
Chapter Eleven
Chapter Twelve
Chapter Thirteen
Chapter Fourteen
Chapter Fifteen
Chapter Sixteen
Chapter Seventeen
Chapter Eighteen
Chapter Nineteen
Chapter Twenty
Chapter Twenty-One
Chapter Twenty-Two
Chapter Twenty-Three
Chapter Twenty-Four
Chapter Twenty-Five
Chapter Twenty-Six
Chapter Twenty-Seven

Chapter Twenty-Eight
Chapter Twenty-Nine
Chapter Thirty
Chapter Thirty-One
Chapter Thirty-Two
Chapter Thirty-Three
Chapter Thirty-Four
Chapter Thirty-Five
Chapter Thirty-Six
Chapter Thirty-Seven
Chapter Thirty-Eight
Chapter Thirty-Nine
Chapter Forty
Chapter Forty-One
Chapter Forty-Two
Chapter Forty-Three
Chapter Forty-Four

Murder in the Key of M

To S

CHAPTER ONE

I COULD SEE the stairs needed sweeping from my vantage point behind the counter, sitting in my faux-leather covered office chair. The fact that the stairs leading down to my basement level music store had actually collected dust due to lack of traffic was a little disconcerting to me, to be honest. I can't say I didn't have regular business, usually business was quite brisk. It just seemed that in the last week or so, not a soul in the entire town had broken a string, lost a pick, or needed a guitar repaired in any way. It seemed my bread-and-butter had turned stale and spoiled. But, just like any business, there are always green times and lean times. I don't sweat it. By next week there will be a new batch of teenagers wanting to start a garage band coming in the doors to buy used electrics, amplifiers, and possibly a full drum kit. In fact, I'd been doing the prep work for hiring my first employee. I'd even looked into getting an insurance benefit through a company that catered specifically to small businesses.

Jack's Music is on the basement level of a building on the corner of Main Street and Lang Avenue that I share with a lady upstairs, Sheila Bryant, who runs a pottery shop. The first two years I was in business, she called me Mr. Gulley. While she finally started calling me Jack, I still call her Ms. Bryant. Old habits and all that. We share the ground level entrance on Lang Street to both shops as a primary entrance to my store and a secondary entrance to her shop. She has a primary set of doors on the front of the building, exposing the pottery shop to Main street. This usually means the store upstairs is busier than mine, but I've learned to live with the quiet times downstairs. My business is pretty good! I clear all I need to make, and then some. I have pretty good margins, and I know how to upsell!

I took advantage of the lull and use the time I had wisely. I began cleaning. Dusty stairs included.

Customers used the amps frequently enough that they required little dusting. They were all in a neat row along the wall underneath the assortment of guitars I had hanging prominently on the wall to the back and left of the stairs. The drum kits that were set up in the middle of the space were usually hard to clean due to all the small grooves that were difficult to get into, but were not really as dusty as I had expected them to be, so no biggie. The shelves which held my small supply of music books and tablature over on the opposite end of the room to the stairs were not as lucky. By the time I made it around to the strings, cords, and picks, along with the other random music supplies behind the long counter sitting directly out from the entrance, I was already thinking about using the slowdown in business as an excuse to take a vacation instead.

The guitars needed no cleaning. I kept them well. I always looked at them like beautiful ladies; treat them well and they will stay around for a long time. Unfortunately, none of the actual women in my life ever seemed to. Maybe I was better off. Maybe they were better off.

I had married once before. She was a little crazy. Maybe I drove her there. Sometimes when you're in love, you don't notice that so much. Maybe love makes you crazy, but it was a great kind of crazy.

Her name was Michelle. I remember, in the beginning, how we used to talk about anything for hours on end. We could have great conversations about a bagel. Maybe we were both nuts. I think that having someone who you can be exactly who you are with is what love is all about. If they know you are totally in love with who they truly are, makes being a little nuts just a bonding thing. It wasn't as if she was really crazy. I guess her unique situation gave her a different outlook on things. All I know is cancer sucks.

We had 20 good years together, but it wasn't enough, not for me. I wanted 80 more. A million more. Now I was 46 years old, running a pretty successful business, healthy enough, but no one to share it with. My once dark brown hair and beard was starting to gray, and I was starting to look forward to my occasional visits from my son Trevor more than I used to. Family was becoming more important to me. I just needed to catch up with some of them.

Trevor was an artist when it came to photography. Something he got from his mother. He'd been published a couple of times, and I was always a proud papa!

"Jack?" I heard a distinctly male voice say, along with the familiar jingles of the bells on the door up the stairs as someone came into the shop. It shook me out of my memories of my sweet Michelle and and of my son, Trevor. I turned to look and see a man in somewhat unkempt shirt and tie coming down the stairs who, unfortunately, didn't look like he wanted to buy a guitar.

"Jack Gulley?" he said with a pleasant, yet authoritative voice.

"Yeah. That's me. What can I do for you?" I said, putting the can of furniture polish and dust cloth I was holding down and extending my right hand. He took his hand out of his pocket and gave a slight look of surprise, as if he had just remembered the pleasantries of meeting a person who wasn't a possible perpetrator for the first time. By now, I could plainly see the badge of the detective on his hip.

"Nice to meet you." He said, sounding a little unrehearsed with the almost clichéd exchange.

"My name is Detective Mark Tuttle, HGPD." Harrows Gate police department was short on real detectives, mostly because we aren't really a big enough town to merit more than a couple of them, at most. His chest puffed just a little when he said it, like he wore his title as a badge of honor. As he should. He didn't seem arrogant or overly proud, he seemed like a man who took pride in his work. I can appreciate that.

"Nice meeting you as well." I said. "What brings you to my little music shop? Can I interest you in guitar lessons?" I asked, joshing him a little.

"Oh! No, nothing like that..." Detective Tuttle said, looking around the shop as if it were the first time he realized he was in a music store, surrounded by instruments. "I'm actually here to see if you can help me with something. Let me get straight to the point. I was just assigned a case that involves a musical instrument that you might remember. It seems you had a hand in procuring the thing for the University sometime back. A rare piano."

He produced a photo of a young woman standing next to a large and beautiful grand piano. I knew the photo and the piano well. They had indeed involved me in assisting the local University's music director in procuring this gorgeous instrument. It was a pristine vintage Bösendorfer piano. One of the original 290's. Those pianos were the first to offer 97 keys instead of the standard 88 you get on a regular piano. They originally ordered the Bösendorfer 290 as a custom keyboard for the composer Ferruccio Busoni in 1909 because he was trying to transcribe a particularly broad piece of organ music. Transcribing organ music to piano can be tricky because the organ has more keys than a piano. Most Grand Pianos are beautiful, but this one was exquisite. In fact, as far as anyone knew, that piano might have actually been the original one delivered to Busoni. It wouldn't have surprised me.

"Yes, sir, I know that beauty! And I'm not talking about the girl." I said a little cheekily. I noticed he wasn't smiling. Well, nobody said I was a stand-up comedian. I changed the subject.

"So what seems to be the issue with the piano, detective?" I asked.

"Someone stole it last night. The University's in a panic." he said. "I was hoping you might be able to shed a little light on the subject of how, and why, someone would steal such a piano."

I think my jaw may have dropped. I was a little taken aback by the idea of the Bösendorfer being stolen. "I could certainly understand the motive. I mean, retail for a new Imperial was most recently valued at over two hundred and fifty thousand dollars. That particular piano was an original. Priceless. But that poses its own problems, doesn't it? I mean, where would they sell it?" I asked.

"I was hoping you could tell me." Said the detective.

"Honestly, I'm not sure who would have the resources to buy a piano of that caliber around here. Around here, anywhere near here, or anywhere not near here, for that matter. I mean, the piano was a donation to the University. I doubt that even the board of the University could come up with enough cash to buy that piano outright. It would be a deep cut in the budget at the very least, and... anyway." I said contemplatively. "But I might talk to some friends of mine in the business. I know a couple of guys acting as agents in major instrument sales, auctions, etcetera. Maybe they could have heard of something."

"Listen, Jack is it? Would you mind coming over to the university and looking at a few things? Maybe you might see something the could shed a little more light on the subject for us." Tuttle said.

I thought for a moment. This was a little unusual. I assumed that a police detective wouldn't want a music shop owner to help in an investigation. "Why do you need my help?"

"To be honest, the intricacies of historic pianos are a little beyond me. I know when to ask for help." he said. "Just stay with me, don't wander around the crime scene, and ask me before you touch *anything*."

"Got it. Well, not much is going on here. I suppose I could close up shop for the day a little early." I said, as I reached for my jacket and keys. I flipped the switch, and the lights went out as we headed out the door to the shop.

"Mrs. Bryant?" I yelled upstairs. "I'm going out for the rest of the day. Can you lock up on your own tonight?"

I grew up an army brat, moving from base to base. My father was a patriot through and through. He had me address everyone formally. It's stuck with me to this day. Mrs. Bryant owned the building, so I've always addressed her formally. Always have, always will.

Sheila Bryant stuck her head around the corner, her face covered in ceramic dust. "Business that slow, Jack?" she asked.

"No, it's not that... well, uh, actually, *today* it is. But that's not why I'm leaving. I'll see you tomorrow, okay?" I was a little embarrassed at my admission, but there was no reason to be dishonest.

With pleasantries complete, the detective and I headed off to the university and to whatever clues there might be to find. Tuttle's car was a burgundy Caddie. Not a nice, shiny, new one, but an old, faded, crappy one. It was the size of a boat, though most Caddies are, and the hubcaps were those wire-spoke type that are hopelessly out of fashion today. I'm not sure how he had kept this car running. After so long, you have to either be willing to throw down the cash to keep a car roadworthy, or just accept that it's time for it to take the expressway across the rainbow bridge. Not judging, though. My definition of a good car is if it can get me from point A to point B without stopping unexpectedly somewhere in-between, so I have no place to talk.

I opened the door to Detective Tuttle's car and was met with a sound that would make bats fly off course. I sank down into the car seat and waited, listening to the air hiss through the faux leather.

Tuttle got into the car and immediately reached toward the dash.

He shuffled through a folder that was sitting on his dashboard and pulled out a sheet of paper that looked like some sort of police paperwork, and handed it to me. While I was trying to figure out which side was up, Tuttle began explaining it to me.

"Here, this is Autumn Bayless' account of what she knew about the piano. I had some uniforms go ask her some questions after I saw her picture. Thought she might know something. Turns out, not so much. You can read that report for what it's worth. She talks about the details of the piano in there. Might mean more to you than to me. I don't know. Give it a read and see."

I politely scanned over the report, but wasn't really reading it. Then I noticed we weren't moving.

I looked over at Tuttle and saw him staring back at me. Then I realized he was waiting for me to put on my seat belt.

"Oh." I said.

I did so, and we were off.

I have to admit that the car rode like a dream. It felt like we were gliding on air in that old Caddie. I think I remembered my grandparents having an old boat of a car like the detective's, or maybe it just seemed that way to me as a child. Either way, this old jalopy that Tuttle was cruising us around in was heavy enough to keep the ride smooth as butter, but could also drive right through a more recently made vehicle without losing speed. It felt safe, I'll admit, though I wouldn't want to be driving a Prius if the Caddie came plowing into me in an accident.

Harrows Gate University was coming up on our left. I was excited to see an actual crime scene! Maybe it wasn't a murder like you see on CSI, but I was eager to see how a proper investigation worked.

CHAPTER TWO

AS WE PULLED up to the University and around the curve of the main entrance, we went up a short road to the right. When we stopped the car, we were at the rear entrance of Devon Hall, the building that used to house the Bösendorfer. The aged brick building with original windows, built in the last part of the 19th century, majestic and beautiful, was a fusion of old world craftsmanship and modern style inside.

"When they moved it into the auditorium, it took three people, a piano jack, plus a specially built dolly." I said to Tuttle. "I can't see how one person by themselves could move something that weighs over twelve-hundred pounds." It was really hitting me now, that the Bösendorfer was gone, and that a piece of musical history could potentially be lost forever.

Tuttle seemed to mumble something, more to himself than to me. A complaint about the headache that was rolling over his now furrowed brow. A uniformed officer met us at the rear door of the building as we got out of the now parked burgundy Crown Vic.

"More than likely, it had to have been somebody that had a key," said a medium build, sort of dull-looking cop. Conner Garrison was his name. I remembered him from high school. We used to get into the most philosophical debates over which was better training for life after school, music or football. Turns out neither of us was right or wrong. We just made do.

"There were no signs of forced entry. Security noticed the piano was missing when they opened the building this morning at 8:00 a.m." Conner looked to me for a fast glance, nodded in acknowledgment, then looked back to the ever furrowed brow of the good detective standing next to me.

"Any idea's on how they could have moved a piano of this size and weight yet, Conner?" Tuttle asked.

"I'm honestly shocked they could manage to get it off the stage in one piece! I saw that piano about a year ago when I was here for a show. That thing was massive!" Conner mused aloud.

"Thank's, Conner. Canvas the area and see if anyone saw anything last night." Tuttle said.

"You got it." said Conner, and he was off, heading toward the row of student housing down the hill from the auditorium. I watched him as he strolled up to the students sitting in lawn chairs outside the buildings and started asking questions, and I tried to read their body language, which was a moot point. They looked at the officer like he was speaking in gibberish. Maybe he would have more luck with the next group.

"Gulley!" Tuttle barked. I jumped a little. I was so distracted by watching the officer question the students that I had forgotten to follow Tuttle into the building. He was holding the door open for me now. "Are you coming?" he asked.

"Er- uh- yeah." I said, coming around the car and through the door. "Sorry about that."

Once inside the auditorium, we walked straight up and onto the stage. "I remember bringing the piano into the auditorium through the back bay doors right over there." I said, pointing to the large double doors at the back of the stage. "I assume they'd have to have taken the piano out that way, too."

Tuttle moved to the double doors and began inspecting them. He was looking at the lock on the doors when we heard a rather loud voice coming from the front.

"Where is the lead investigator?"

Storming down the aisle of the theater was a rather frumpy-looking, middle-aged woman with purple hair. The dichotomy of the frumpiness and the odd hair color choice made for quite the spectacle, shouting aside. She had our attention.

As the perturbed woman shoved a uniformed officer out of her way, while she almost audibly ground her teeth, Tuttle came around to find out what the commotion was. The detective put his hand up, motioning for the woman to stop, as if he were directing traffic. She stopped in her tracks, but scowled at Tuttle and narrowed her eyes.

"What are you doing? Where is my piano? Why are you just standing around??"

This was the gist of the litany that came out of her puckered face, alongside and intermingled with a slew of profanity, the likes of which I'll spare you.

"Hold it right there, ma'am. Why don't you just calm down and tell me exactly who you are before I answer any of your questions?" Tuttle said. There was that authoritative voice again. The two stood nose-to-nose for what seemed like an eternity, neither breaking their gaze. Finally, the woman broke out of her scowl, letting out a loud sigh.

"Oh, for God's sake. My name is Dr. Brenda Clark. I'm the Music Director for the University. Now where is my blasted piano?"

Tuttle inhaled and looked up a little, seeming to put it all together in his head. "I see. Dr. Clark, we're doing everything we can to get your piano back...."

"And what in the blazes of the down below is that exactly?" Clark said heatedly, cutting the detective off mid-sentence.

"Well, for one thing, we've enlisted some help in finding the piano. This is Jack Gulley, the gentleman who assisted the University in procuring the Bösendorfer." he said, while gesturing in my general direction.

"Hello. I just hope I can help somehow." I said sheepishly, trying not to draw the ire of Clark. She just glared at me, so I counted myself as lucky.

"I would have hoped that you would have something to show for your efforts by now. Don't you have any leads?" Clark said, sounding less angry now and more perturbed.

"I assure you, we have only just started our investigation, but we will find this piano as quickly as we can." Tuttle said, like he was trying to soothe a child coming down from a tantrum.

"You better! Sooner rather than later, too! I can't afford to lose that piano! You have to understand the pressure I'm under. The board only authorized the funds to pay for the piano on the express condition that it remain a part of the University's collection of antiquities." Clark said, once again getting fired up, muttering something about "the board" and "funds" as she wiped her palms on her skirt, scanning her eyes across the room nervously. Fortunately for us, Clark took this opportunity to turn on her heel and storm off the stage, still mumbling and finally raising her voice with a "For God's sake!". She headed behind the curtains and down the stairs in the back hallway that led down to the basement level of the building where mostly offices were located, by my recollection of the place from years ago.

"Yeah, we'll get right on that." Tuttle said under his breath.

"Well, she was a bright ray of sunshine, wasn't she?" I said, trying to lighten the mood.

"Huh? Oh! Yeah, right." Tuttle shook his head and shrugged his shoulders, brushing the whole interchange off. "Jack? Do you remember Clark from when you delivered the piano?"

I had to think for a moment, but I had to admit that I didn't remember her. "No. I don't." I said. "Sorry."

"You'd remember her if you had met her. Don't you think?" Tuttle replied with a touch of a grin.

"I'd have to agree with you there." I said. We both chuckled to ourselves a little.

*****

As the afternoon wore on, I spread out my search for anything helpful to the police, to the rest of the auditorium. I found nothing that made a difference in the slightest, as far as I could tell. The only thing I could find was a couple of programs for a concert held in the auditorium just the night before. It was apparently a fairly fancy event. The pianist was the very girl from the picture Tuttle had come to my shop with. I wondered if she may have seen something that could help.

I took the program and stuffed it in my back pocket. As I

headed to the stage, I waved to Tuttle.

"I was going to ask if you've talked to the girl from the photo?" I asked him.

"Autumn Baylor. Yeah, I had some uniformed officers talk to her. Why?" Tuttle asked.

"I thought she might know something is all. She was apparently performing last night in this hall. Maybe she saw something?" I said.

Tuttle shrugged and put his hands out. "I don't see what it would hurt."

"Good!" I said, trying to think about what questions I might have for her. "I really think she would have a wonderful insight on this."

Tuttle stared at me with a distant look in his eye, like he had gotten lost in a thought he couldn't shake.

"What's wrong?" I asked.

"You know, after this visit to Ms. Baylor, I'd like to talk to that Clark lady again, God help me." Tuttle said with a grimace.

"Glutton for punishment?" I asked.

"Maybe, but I feel like she might have a little more info that could help if she'd just calm down for a second." Tuttle said while reaching for his phone that had just started buzzing.

"Tuttle." He said into the phone as he turned to face the other direction. "Yeah, got it. Thanks." Tuttle pressed the screen with his index finger and turned back to face me. "That was the captain. I have some forms I need to file. I'll tell you what, since we already had an officer take an official statement from Baylor, why don't you talk to her yourself if you like. We have everything we need from her for the time being. If you find out anything pertinent, let me know. Deal?"

"Deal." I said. I was feeling like a sleuth from one of the mystery shows I watched as a kid. Sure, I was no Columbo, but a guy can have fun with the idea of being Sherlock Holmes once in a while. Heck, I'd settle for Jessica Fletcher!

As Tuttle headed down the stairwell to the right of the stage, he ran into Clark, coming from the lower levels. She looked at him with a glare, but this time she tamed the outright hostility to a smolder.

"Ms. Clark, I was actually just coming to speak with you." Tuttle said. Not really a lie, but I'm sure he was hoping to do it on his own terms and not impromptu in a stairwell.

"Doctor." Clark said.

"Excuse me?" Tuttle asked, clearly not catching on that this was her title.

"Doctor Clark. I earned it." Clark said with a rise in her chest and a slight tilt of her nose to the air.

"Er, um, oh. Yes. Doctor Clark." Tuttle said, looking as if he were fighting the urge to roll his eyes.

"Thank you." She said coldly, crossing her arms.

"What I wanted to see you about was to ask if you remember anything from last night that seemed... off. Was anyone here that didn't seem to belong? Out of place?" Tuttle stepped back a little to wait for an answer or to defend himself if need be.

"I'm sure there were no shady-types lurking in the shadows last night when I locked up. I looked the place over myself before leaving. I pride myself in making sure that my hall is spotless." Clark said, tilting the nose up again at the last comment.

"What about Baylor's concert? Did anything happen that might have made you scratch your head?" Tuttle asked.

Clark was getting that look in her eyes again, as if she were about to light into one of her rants.

"Believe me, Detective Tuttle..." she added emphasis to the detective, apparently to show Tuttle how a person is to address someone with a formal title. "I will tell you anything that comes to mind that might assist you in finding my piano. Now please, will you excuse me, Detective Tuttle?"

Clark turned and stormed away without waiting for any such permission.

By the time she had finished speaking, I have to believe we were all grinding our teeth as hard as she was. With a curt turn, Dr. Clark headed back down the stairwell and out of sight.

"She certainly has a chip on her shoulder, doesn't she?" I

noted as I peeked around the corner.

Tuttle jumped. "Wha...?!? Jack! I thought you went to talk to that girl." Tuttle said with some impatience in his voice.

"Well, I saw you run into Doctor Clark. I wanted to hear what she had to say. Sorry." I replied.

"Well, she seems like a dead end. Not very interested in actually being helpful." Tuttle said. "If this ever ends up in court, I'll recommend they treat her as a hostile witness." I couldn't help but believe Tuttle was only half-joking.

"Well, I'm off to see Baylor. I'll let you know what I find out." I said. And with that, I headed for the doors at the front of the hall and out into the University quadrangle.

Tuttle just watched as I reached the doors and pulled on the large brass handles, swinging the tall, carved wood works of art open and slipping out. You could say what you want about Dr. Clark, but the University was a beautiful place. I would have liked to have attended this school back when I was younger, but I was too busy picking my guitar. My education came from clubs, honky-tonks, and county fairs; anywhere they would pay a man to play his music. A real-world education, as they say. Still, I had always been fascinated with the idea of going to college. Wondered what if and all that? I just never got around to following that dream. Maybe some day. Just maybe I'll feel the bug bite hard enough to scratch the itch. Until that day comes, I'm satisfied with my music shop. It pays the bills and brings me satisfaction that I get to spend my working day, if not living out my musical dreams, helping others start their journey.

But now I was finding my journey seeming a little more adventurous. The excitement of an actual crime scene and the idea of looking for clues and interviewing potential witnesses enamored me. I didn't want it to end. And it had just started.

CHAPTER THREE

TUTTLE HEADED OUT the back door of Devon Hall and out to his car, a Burgundy 1987 Cadillac El Dorado. Tuttle didn't care what Jack said. This car was a classic. As Tuttle lifted the handle, his door squeaked obnoxiously as he opened it; the seat cushion letting out an audible whoosh as the springs gave out a short, slightly rusty sounding scream when Tuttle sank into the driver's side. The smell of his car was that of old cheeseburger and musk. He wasn't a smoker, but somehow one would almost feel like they could smell cigar as well, perhaps from a previous owner.

The questioning of Dr. Clark had not gone as well as he had expected, so Tuttle looked into his questions about last night's concert himself. He headed to the dorms to see what information he could glean by questioning the people closest to the campus hub of activity, the students.

As Tuttle drove along the outer road of the campus leading up the hill to the residence halls, he saw Jack walking in that direction as well.

Jack, you're probably barking up the wrong tree, brother, he thought to himself.

Tuttle admired that Jack wanted to get so invested in the process. He reminded Tuttle of himself when he first started the academy, all spit and vinegar, as they say. Jack had good instincts but needed training. If Jack were younger, Tuttle would suggest he go to the police academy.

But that was just it. He hadn't gone to the academy. He wasn't a cop. As much as he admired his energy, Jack wasn't supposed to be getting involved in this. His role was over, and that was that.

Tuttle made a mental note to talk to Jack later, say thanks for the help, but the actual police work is for real police.

Tuttle nodded in agreement with himself, and he pumped the brakes slightly as his car slowed.

He could see he was coming up on the student housing tract on campus. The dormitories all looked exactly alike, two-story brick and white trimmed buildings, first floor residence doors on the front with open stairwells in the middle to get to the second-floor rooms.

As Tuttle got out of his car, he pulled his long, black felt coat around him as the fall wind blew a gust that chilled him and rustled the trees overhead, peppering crispy leaves down onto the sidewalk in front of him. The students here should be able to shed some light on the missing piano. The dorms face the hill that Devon Hall sits on. Tuttle was certain that someone had to have seen something.

As he stepped up to the first door and knocked, he straightened his tie and tucked in his shirt. He was not usually much for shirt and tie in his private life, but the department had its dress code for detectives.

The door opened and a boy, who looked all of about 19 years old, stood before him.

"Yeah?" the young man said.

"Detective Mark Tuttle, Harrow's Gate police." Tuttle said, flashing his badge and ID. "I wanted to ask you a few questions. Is that OK?"

"Sure. About what?" the boy asked, looking like an animal that had suddenly found itself cornered.

"For the record, could I ask your name?" Tuttle asked.

"Reggie. Reggie Blake." He replied, somewhat awkwardly.

"I was wondering if you had seen anything last night, up on the hill there. Devon Hall?" Tuttle asked.

"Why? Did something happen? Was somebody shot?!?" Reggie said, craning his neck around Tuttle to see if there was a scene.

"Uh, eh, no? No guns involved, so far as I know. There's been

19

no shots fired by anyone. Someone stole the piano that was in the concert hall." Tuttle told Reggie.

"Oh. Okay." Reggie replied, sounding somewhat disappointed and seeming to relax a little now. Tuttle raised an eyebrow, literally and internally. Tuttle just shook his head slightly and returned to his list of questions.

"Well, there was a big, white truck up there for about 30 minutes. Is that what you mean?" Reggie volunteered before Tuttle could get on to the next question. Reggie looked quizzically at Tuttle, looking for some hint that he had seen something that would blow the case out of the water. Tuttle just looked back at Reggie.

"The truck you saw, were there any markings?" Tuttle asked calmly.

"Yeah." Reggie said and then smiled, hoping he had helped tremendously.

After a moment of awkward silence, Tuttle asked Reggie, "Well, were the markings anything you could make out?"

"No." Reggie said.

"OK.... Did you see where the truck went when they left?" Tuttle was feeling like talking to Reggie may have been both a blessing and a curse. He saw something, true, but it's not entirely clear if Reggie even knew what he saw. As a bonus, Reggie was giving him a headache as well.

"Well... thank you, Reggie. You have been a great help." Tuttle said and turned on his heels in order to return to his car.

That was totally useless, he thought.

"Um, Detective Tuttle? I think the guys that were around the truck were wearing green coveralls. Does that help?" Reggie said uncertainly.

Tuttle stopped. A grin rose on his face, ever so slightly. "Yes, Reggie. Possibly. That may just help. Thanks."

Tuttle wasn't sure that it would help at all, but who knows?

When Tuttle got back in his car, he pulled out his cell phone and called into the station.

"Hey, Sarah. Do me a favor, canvas for moving companies

with white trucks and where the employees wear coveralls, say, in the 50-mile radius range. Got it? Thanks. I owe you one."

Tuttle started his car and headed back to the station.

On his way, Tuttle stopped at his favorite campus burger joint, Burger Box, and got his usual combo and milkshake.

Tuttle had a history with, nay, a love affair with cheeseburgers. It started when he was a boy, and he can still remember the first time he smelled his father's grill light up. The charcoal briquets flaming up and cooking down to a white ash on the outside, radiating the scorching heat that added a sizzling sear to the round, pink patties that his father brought out on a tray. The smell and the sounds were delightful, and the slices of Swiss and cheddar that were laid on the meat just a minute or two before the patties went on a slightly toasted bun; just long enough to make it melt and possibly, if you're lucky, bubble. A little onion, pickle and mustard, and maybe a slice of tomato and a lettuce leaf... perfection. After that, Tuttle never met a burger he didn't like.

Just as he took his first bite, his radio chirped, "Mark, you better not be eating that crap from Burger Box again. That stuff will stop your heart." Linda Raines, the HGPD Medical Examiner, said sounding condescending and authoritative at the same time.

"You know me, Linda. I'm having a salad and a bottle of flavored water." Tuttle said with a large bite of juicy burger in his cheek and dabbing a wad of fries in ketchup.

"If you're eating a salad, I'm walking the runway next week in Paris." Linda quipped.

Tuttle just grinned while he chewed his meal. "Alright, Raines, what have you got for me?"

"I have those results you wanted for the Swinson case, and the bloodwork for the toxicology report on Mick Lowell came back negative." Linda said.

"Okay. I'll file them when I get back. I'm going to finish my... salad.... And I'll be back at the station soon." Tuttle said.

Tuttle finally got back to his first love, the cheeseburger.

CHAPTER FOUR

I SAW TUTTLE drive down the hill towards some student housing. I know I'm not a professional detective like him, but in my humble opinion, he's barking up the wrong tree.

The trek across campus was beautiful indeed. The lush, green fir trees, the crisp oak, elm and sycamore leaves on the ground, crunching under my feet as I walked. I hadn't been to the University for quite a while and hadn't fully remembered how beautiful this campus actually was. It was fall, and so the trees had all taken on beautiful colors of gold, yellow, red, and orange. The leaves that had already fallen from the trees seemed to call up to their brothers and sisters to join them every time the breeze picked up, sending a rustling sound into the air. The air had a crisp, cool note to it that filled my lungs and gave a pep to my step.

As I strolled along the path towards the dorm that was listed on the copy of the statement that Tuttle gave me, I wondered if Baylor had mentioned anything in the report that might give me any ideas about what could have happened to the piano after the concert last night.

As I scanned over the report, actually reading it this time, I realized her statement was nothing short of bedtime reading. Nothing stood out that would give me any clues to what might have happened to the piano. She went into great detail about when she got home, her bedtime routine, and what she had for a late dinner.

I almost fell asleep walking. I hoped she was more interesting in person than in this report. It occurred to me at that moment that I didn't remember Autumn, not really. I remember taking the picture with her next to the Bösendorfer, but I was just told to stand here, smile, and next. I remember exchanging pleasantries, but no genuine conversation.

Back then, Michelle was pretty sick at the time and all I wanted to do was get back home to her.

I buzzed the bell of the front door of the dormitory that Autumn Baylor lived in. A moment later, the door opened and a young lady with short blonde hair looked back at me while chewing a wad of gum that had to be several pieces big or, at the very least, a huge wad of Big League Chew.

"Good evening. I was looking for Autumn Baylor. My name is Jack Gulley. I'm assisting the police in finding the missing piano. Is she available?"

"I thought she already talked to the police." The blonde girl chewing the still-impressive wad of gum said.

"I'm sorry, I didn't catch your name?" I said.

"I didn't give it, Kojak." She said.

"It's just Jack, actually." I couldn't believe I was falling into this. "A few years ago I was here when they originally delivered the piano to the University. Autumn was there for the big day. I wanted to see if I could ask her a few questions."

After just staring at me while chewing that huge wad of gum for what seemed like the longest ten seconds of my life, she looked over her shoulder and yelled into the house. "AUTUMN! SOME GUY IS HERE ABOUT THE PIANO!"

"What does he want? I already talked to the police." I heard her yell back.

"IT'S AN OLD-MAN COP YOU DATED A COUPLE OF YEARS AGO." the blonde girl with no name called up the stairs.

"Wait! What? I never said I dated her! And I'm not a cop! I just said I was here when they delivered the piano!" I said with a little sound of shock in my voice. "And I'm not *that* old, either." I said under my breath. The blonde gum-chewer just shrugged and rolled her eyes and walked away. She was chuckling to herself. Obviously, she'd just been amusing herself by getting a rise out of me. After hearing feet stomping down the stairs at a speed I was sure was about to turn into someone actively falling down the steps, a demure girl with jet black hair and horn-rimmed glasses to match was standing in front of me with a look on her face that had a mix of confusion and revulsion along with a hint of annoyance and perhaps a peppering of outright disgust.

"We never dated. I would never…" she started saying, but I cut her off before she hurt my feelings.

"No, I understand. I never said we dated. Or I was a cop… I simply said I was here when they delivered the Bösendorfer. I remembered you and thought I'd see if you could remember anything else since you spoke with the police?"

"Wait. You're not with the police?" she asked.

"Er, well, no. Not exactly. I'm consulting for the police." I said. It did not impress her.

"I found a program from your concert last night and wanted to see if you remembered anything that seemed out of place during or after the show." I added while pulling the program from my pocket.

Autumn just stared at me, slack-jawed, much like the blonde girl who has no known identity but loves her gum.

"Okay, just level with me. Is there anything you can tell me that might help find the piano? Knowing how much it meant to you and Dr. Clark to get that piano, I'm assuming you want us to get it back." I said, hoping to appeal to her sensibilities and passion for music and, more precisely, fantastically exquisite pianos. Instead, she just said "No. Sorry." And shut the door.

I knocked on the door again. My favorite gum-chewing blonde answered again. "She said she doesn't want to talk anymore." she said, gripping a slim graphic design textbook. I realized, not being a police officer, and could not ask to see her identification, I had no recourse and did the only thing I could do.

"Jessica?" I asked. "Rebecca? Lisa??"

She just stared blankly and chewed like a cow on its cud. I just turned and walked away. "Was I even close?" I asked aloud after her.

I shrugged, holding my hands out, palms up.

After giving up on learning the true identity of the blonde with gum, I headed back across campus to check in with Tuttle and see if I could be of any more help. Along the sides of the walkway I was following, there were rocks sticking out of the ground that the various Greek organizations had painted. Whether the rocks were naturally occurring or someone planted them there, I wasn't sure, but they'd been there so long it didn't appear one could tell the difference. I was hoping to see the stone of the fraternity I pledged in college, Gamma Alpha Beta. Though I didn't find one, I got a pleasant flood of memories. I remembered, most of all, meeting Michelle for the first time. She was in my fraternity's sister sorority, the Kappa Pi Thetas. We hit it off immediately at an off-campus get-together. We may have had a little too much to drink and hopped in my car and sped off, laughing our tails off, while our brothers and sisters all yelled at us for driving at all. Like I said, we were crazy. But I needed to keep my head in the game today. There was a piano missing, and I needed to be of help to Tuttle and his band of merry cops, so that meant not getting caught up in my own issues.

Upon making it back to the front steps of Devon Hall, I noticed the police were packing up and were all getting back into their cars. Tuttle came through the front doors and immediately saw me and headed my way.

"Well, Jack? Did you learn anything new?" he said, sweeping the sides of his long coat back and inserting his hands into his pockets.

"Well, not sure really." I said it in a tone like a dog with its tail between its legs might have.

"Meh. I wasn't expecting much." Tuttle said as he fiddled with the badge on his hip. "Don't sweat it. Police work is best left to the police."

I have to admit, that stung a bit. My stint of playing Sherlock Holmes was short and ill-fated. I knew it, and Tuttle knew it. Heck, Tuttle probably knew it before it started. I decided that I'd be better off getting back to my shop. Back to my guitars, my passion, and where I belong.

"C'mon, Jack", Tuttle said as kindly as he could, but in my head it sounded as patronizing as you could get. "Let's get you home."

We pulled open the doors to Tuttle's car and got in. The leather seats crackled and the springs underneath squeaked, as usual, as we settled our weights into the car. I could distinctly smell what reminded me of fast food. The wadded up bag from Burger Box on the floor board confirmed my sniffer's detective skills. At least my nose was a decent detective. Tuttle started the engine and slowly pulled out of the space. I didn't say much on the ride home, but I was thinking. And for once, it wasn't just about Michelle.

And now I wanted a cheeseburger.

CHAPTER FIVE

TUTTLE'S CAR CRUISED up to my house a little after 8:00 p.m. I got out of his car and he handed me his business card.

"If you think of anything else that might help, let me know. You were a great help today, Gulley." Tuttle said.

"I will. Not sure I was much help, though."

"Listen, Jack. If everybody in this town were willing to help investigations, the way you seem to want to help us, our crime rate would be almost nothing. You did well."

I had to admit, Tuttle saying that gave me a sense of pride.

"Thanks." I said and closed his car door, then headed to my front porch.

My mind was racing from the day. I kept thinking about the piano and the hall. How could a grand piano disappear from a college building like that, on the same night as they performed a concert on that very piano, no less? And how could no one have seen anything?

I started thinking about what I heard from the police while we were at Devon Hall. Whoever took the piano must have had a key. Or was at least great at picking locks. There had been a concert that night, so it had to have happened after that. But when was the concert? I remembered putting that program in my back pocket and pulled it out.

I was immediately surprised to see that Fantasia in C Minor was the first selection for the night. In fact, the "in C Minor" part is a bit of a misnomer. To say that Mozart wrote the piece in C Minor is like saying the dictionary is about the letter A. That piece of music may start in C Minor, but the thing is all over the place. Only two keys are actually notated, though. Mozart wrote most of that piece in accidentals, where the composer changes the individual notes to flat or sharp as needed. Altogether, this thing has something like eight key signatures!

At any rate, I felt it was a rather heavy piece for a small-town school like ours. But then again, Autumn Baylor was no casual pianist. A true prodigy, as I recall. She was top of her class in piano, starting back when she was just a small girl in school. I remember hearing all the razzle and dazzle from the powers that be at the University back when the piano was being delivered.

"Baylor was a child prodigy, you know?" they said, "She was playing by the time she was five!"

I looked at the program again.

HARROW'S GATE UNIVERSITY

SENIOR PIANO RECITAL

By

Autumn Savannah Baylor

DEVON HALL

WEDNESDAY MAY 25, 2016 At 7:00 P.M. O'clock

Fantasia in C Minor..Mozart

There were a few more music selections listed. Some I knew well, and a few I didn't. I figured that the concert was around 2 hours if you included all the music pieces and a minimum of chatter between pieces. So if they stole the piano after 9:00 p.m., and assuming it was probably after 10:00 p.m. by the time all the hullabaloo dispersed... nothing. I had nothing. The theft occurred after 10:00 p.m. And before 8:00 a.m., before the opening of the building. Ten full hours to account for. I was absolutely going nuts at the fact that not a soul saw anything. Why was this bothering me so much? It wasn't my problem. It wasn't even my piano!

The next night, after putting in a day's work at the music store, my son Trevor, being the art lover he is, of many kinds of art at that, drug me to a play. Now, this play was one of those interpretive plays that mean different things to different people. The first half of the play was quite interesting from a purely "this must be what being on psychotropic drugs must feel like" point of view.

At some point, I must have finally fallen prey to the craziness of it all. I was actually interested in what was happening on the stage. I knew I was probably just in some weird mood that miraculously lined up with the excitement of live theater, the crowd, and whatever the heck the story we were watching unfold was supposed to be, but I was engrossed in the play. Like watching a favorite TV show. Especially if you were into terrible TV. There was a girl who was standing on the stage. I didn't recognize the girl; I wondered if she was local. She was very young, maybe six years old. She was pulling a small wooden chest, like the ones they used to have when I was a kid, made of cheap wood with simple brass hinges. The girl was having trouble, like the box was very heavy, although it was just a tiny toy box. She stopped pulling and looked at the chest for a moment, and then she pulled out an iPhone. That got a few chuckles from the audience, though I'm not sure that was the intent. She scrolled and tapped a few times, obviously looking for something on the phone, then she put the phone away and just... stood there. It was surreal. She didn't move or blink, or anything. It was as if she was some sort of video game character, paused on the screen, or stage in this case.

I was looking at the girl on the stage, waiting for her to move, to blink, or anything really, when from out of the surrounding darkness four large men walked out of the shadows, all dressed in coveralls. They were moving in slow motion like those performers you see on the street, simulating slow motion in films. The girl, who had, thankfully, started moving like a normal kid again, was skipping around the men. When she stopped in front of the men, she pointed to the wooden chest on the floor of the stage in front of the men. All the men looked at the chest, still in slow motion, and without seeming to intentionally ever really move into place, the men were each eventually holding a different corner of the chest, and lifted it slowly to waist level. The girl turned around and walked off, out of the light and into the darkness somewhere off of the stage. The men all followed in the mind-numbingly slow manner they had come onto the stage, and the chest disappeared into the darkness with them.

Then I made a short, but magnificently audible gasp.

Not that the incredible, deep meaning that the writer of this stage presentation had been meaning to convey had emotionally struck me, or even that I had found the dramatic depth of character the young girl had apparently tried to emote through her incredibly dramatic pointing at the simple wooden box. No, nor was I gasping about the incredible performances by the four knuckleheads and the coveralls. Nope, I was gasping because something had occurred to me. Something had occurred to me while watching this stupid, and if I may be blunt, ridiculously terrible, play that my son had somehow tricked me into going to.

I was so excited to share this information with Tuttle that my feet were bouncing and I was wringing my hands while sitting in my seat.

When I glanced over, it was to see Trevor widely smiling, apparently enthusiastic about my possible great appreciation for the artistic presentation before us. I didn't care, though. I was on to something. Admittedly, I was smiling, and Trevor seemed happy. That didn't happen too often anymore. Not since Michelle died. I decided not to split hairs and took it at face value. Besides, Trevor had Michelle's smile, and seeing that smile again warmed my heart. I wasn't about to say anything that would jeopardize that moment.

As the play ended and the house lights came up, illuminating the people in the gallery, I firmly squeezed my son's shoulder, stood, and applauded with the rest of the audience as the cast of this absolute travesty of a play took their final bows.

CHAPTER SIX

AFTER WALKING HOME from the, quite frankly, weirdest play I can remember having seen in recent memory, I took a mental note because it had made me realize something that hadn't occurred to me before. I think I had figured out how they had moved the piano. I couldn't figure out the whole 'little girl dragging a box on a string' thing yet. At least from the play point of view, but I was sure on to something now that it had made me realize that whoever stole the Bösendorfer wasn't a professional thief, but I'd bet my left hand that they got some professional help!

I unlocked the door to my house and stepped inside, shutting the door behind me. As I sorted through the mail, tossing the various pieces of junk mail, sales postcards, and bulk rate letters in the trash, setting the bills on the table to look at later when I thought having an anxiety attack might be more palatable, I saw my bed down the hall, and I could feel it calling for me.

I slipped into my sleep pants and just kept my day's tee-shirt on and slid in-between the sheets. The cool cotton brushed across my feet and I pulled up my covers to my chin, closing my eyes and taking in a deep, controlled breath.

I must have fallen asleep almost instantly.

The next morning, after I shook the sleep out of my head and did the usual morning things, I got dressed and headed to my kitchen. After I had some breakfast, I forgot about the play I had seen with Trevor. I was ready to concentrate on more important things, my store more precisely. My poor shop had been a little neglected by me, as of late. I had a truck coming in today with some new Les Paul guitars and a new model of a bass guitar that Yamaha was putting on the market in a few months. I was getting a pre-release model to show off for pre-orders.

If that all wasn't exciting enough, Trevor had sent me an email this morning telling me that when he got home last night, he had news waiting for him. He found out that his photographs were going to be in a new gallery. We made plans for him to come over for lunch today, and I was ready to see some of his new pictures. Trevor is a photographer with a lot of talent and loves nature photography. He has several pictures hanging in galleries in Knoxville and Chattanooga. My hands are too shaky for photography. All I can seem to capture is blurry pictures that look more appropriate for one of those "Is it a Big Foot" shows on T.V. He told me he was bringing a new set of photographs that were being placed in a gallery in Pigeon Forge. I just hoped he didn't want to discuss the play.

I have never been a more proud poppa. The first day he came by the shop and showed me his first gallery acceptance letter, I was about to burst with pride! His mother had passed the year before. I told him she would have been even more proud than I was. I saw a tear welling in his eye and a small smile on his face as he lowered his head. I don't know if that was what set me off, or if it was the joint realization that his mother was not here for this monumental day. For a moment, we both just sat in silence. When we came to ourselves again, we went to eat. I honestly don't remember where we went now. It didn't matter. It started a tradition, though. Now, whenever Trevor gets into a new gallery, we go for lunch. It lets us sort of celebrate with each other, and we always toast Michelle.

On my way to the store, I was coming around the corner and into the parking lot when I remembered the curious thing about the play I had seen last night. I mentioned to Tuttle that there had to have been some equipment used to move the piano. Move the piano. I couldn't shake it. The men in the play. Movers!

I got out of my car and locked the door. I thought about the lock on the door to the university hall. Who all had keys to that door? Tuttle might know. I reached for my phone to call him.

As I pulled my phone out of my pocket and dialed his number, I remembered the little girl, pulling out the what seemed like a huge phone by comparison to her dainty little hands. I wondered what the purpose was of the phone? She ordered the men to come pick up the box, obviously. But what was their...

Movers. With a truck, I bet. Holy crap! I had forgotten to tell Tuttle about it!

I hit Tuttle's number on my phone. It started ringing.

"Detective Mark Tuttle." came the answer on the other end.

"Tuttle! I had a thought. How many people had a key to those doors at the back of the stage?" I asked.

"I think there were four, altogether. Why?"

"Who were they?"

"Well, I'm not sure why it matters, but obviously, Clark had a key. Let's see. Then there was security, and maintenance and they had issued the last one to the Baylor girl. But Clark had her key. Autumn had turned it in the previous week. She would graduate soon and didn't need it anymore. Why do you need to know?"

"Well, let me explain. I saw this play with my son. I think my subconscious was trying to tell me someth..."

"Wait, just wait. Do you mean to tell me you're calling me, asking about potential evidence in an ongoing investigation because of a play you saw?" I could almost hear his eyebrows raising over the phone.

"Well, when you put it that way..." I replied.

"Listen, Jack, I love that you want to help, really I do. But you can't be calling me, slowing me down, when the steam is still rising off this pile-of-crap case they laid on my desk. I don't have time to listen to your play interpretations when I've got a case to solve!" Tuttle rebuked.

"I understand, and I don't mean to slow down your investigation, but I think I can be a great help to you with this." I said to him.

"OK, you want to help? Bring me a plausible explanation along with evidence backing up said explanation, and we'll talk.

If you can do that, great. I'm afraid otherwise I've got to let you go. You know how to reach me." he said and hung up.

But... but I didn't even get to tell him about the movers! At least I think they were movers. They looked like movers. Yeah, definitely movers. That's it! It had to be. I was sure that pros had moved the piano, and now I knew how they did it! Someone had moved the piano with movers! Plain old, run of the mill, sofa and dining room table movers! That was what my "play interpretation senses" were telling me. I had been putting this together in my head all along and finally I realized it!

What was I thinking? Was I going crazy, eh, crazier? I found myself obsessed with figuring out what happened to that piano. And I'd figure it out, one way or another!

I went on into the shop, saying my hello's and good mornings to Sheila upstairs, and made my way downstairs.

I flipped on the lights, turned on the ambiance music, and set up behind the counter in my usual spot. As I settled into my seat, I turned on the iMac sitting at my desk behind the counter and started searching for local piano movers. I was sure Tuttle had already done this, but seeing as how he wasn't talking to me until I had hard evidence, I was on my own.

There weren't that many piano movers in our area, none, in fact. The nearest one was in Knoxville, about 45 minutes away. I figured I'd call them, regardless.

After calling the piano movers and coming up with nothing, I felt like that play wasn't really telling me anything more than a story, made up to entertain me in my theater seat. But something wouldn't let me rest. There was an itch, a fire inside me, that wouldn't let this die. I kept looking.

Calling all the piano movers within 100 miles, I started thinking about other options. Surely, no one would think of using general furniture mover, the guys who come in and throw your couch in the truck, then throw your bed on the couch? Not with a priceless piece of musical history like the Bösendorfer 290? Say it ain't so! I started local and called all the moving companies in town. There had been no moving runs to the

University, and as if that weren't enough, none of the movers were even open at night.

Yes, the time of night was an issue. But this could help. I went back to the computer and googled "24-hour movers". I got two hits. The first one was a dead end. They made very few runs at night. Not one in at least a week, and especially at that hour. They weren't even open. The second one, however, turned out to be pay-dirt.

"Yeah, I sent a couple of our guys down to that neck of the woods the other night. Said they moved some kinda piano or something. They work the night shift. I'd let you talk to one of them right now, otherwise." The dispatcher from Sun and Moon Movers told me.

"Actually, if you could just have one of them call me tonight when they get on shift, that would be great." I said.

The dispatcher agreed, and we hung up the phone.

Reluctantly, I had to step away from my sleuthing to tend to my day job. I had to ring up some customers who had come into my shop while I was on the phone. The kids looked like a couple of country music fans had reproduced to give birth to clones of Clint Black and Johnny Cash.

"You, uh, kids going to start a country music group?" I sounded a little skeptical, I realized.

"Yup. We want to move to Nashville when we get done with high school and become stars." Mr. Cash said.

"And you keep watching the t.v. You'll remember us." Clint said.

If I see these two on t.v. in the future, I'm sure it could only be because they had fell on hard times and got caught robbing a corner convenience store.

After ringing up a pack of strings, six guitar picks, and some guitar polish, I was back on my quest.

Honestly, I was wondering if I even had enough information to call Tuttle back with? Without having spoken to one of those movers, I was afraid that it would all just be too circumstantial. Besides, Tuttle said he wanted evidence. The simple fact that the dispatcher had sent some guys "down to your neck of the woods," as they said, probably did not make up admissible evidence. No, I'd have to dig deeper. This was getting fun!

CHAPTER SEVEN

"DAD!!"

My son's voice startled me. I almost fell off my chair! Time had certainly gotten away from me because Trevor was here and ready to go to lunch.

"Oh, sorry Trevor. You scared the crap out of me! I think I gained a few more gray hairs on that one."

"I gathered; by the girlish yelp you let out and the fact you almost fell on the floor after nearly hitting the ceiling." Trevor quipped. "And speaking of yelps, what did you think about the play last night?"

"Ha-ha. Hilarious. Sorry, son, I hadn't realized what time it was." I was trying to move on and avoid speaking ill of the play he had taken me to.

"What are you looking at anyway?" Trevor started leaning over the counter, trying to peek at the screen of my iMac.

"Well, as it just so happens, I am helping the police with a very important case." I said with a hint of pride. From the look on Trevor's face, it did not impress him. But at least I had dodged the play-talk bullet.

"Why do the police need your help with a case?" Trevor sounded like he was accusing me of pulling his leg.

"Do you remember a while back when I helped get that huge grand piano, the Bösendorfer?" I asked. Trevor just nodded affirmatively, pushing his jacket back to shove his hands in his jean pockets. "Well, someone stole it! And now they want my help as a sort of expert in music and the piano." I told Trevor, no doubt beaming with pride. "They came to me." I gave him a little wink.

"Well, anyway, where do you want to get lunch? I was thinking about Alfredo's. You?" Trevor said with a raised brow. He seemed unimpressed with my explanation of what was going on with the police. "They called me." I repeated the last part as if I thought maybe he hadn't caught on.

What's a guy got to do to impress their only son? *Oh well*, I thought. While every father would love to be their son's hero, there were bigger fish to fry right now, or in this case, pasta to boil.

"Italian sounds good. I can always go for pasta! Before we go, though, did you bring the pictures?" I asked. Trevor, being a photographer, was getting ready for a gallery showing in a few weeks and had brought me a few of his photos pieces to see before the show.

"Oh! Yeah. I just brought one of my major pieces. Here you are..." Trevor pulled a manila envelope out of his satchel and laid it on the glass case in front of me. I unwound the string holding the flap shut and pulled out the contents. There were six black and white photos inside. Each picture was of a unique piece of scenery. They were each beautiful in their own right. But then he took the pictures from my hands.

"Here..." he spread the photos on the counter, laying the pictures out in a particular order. And then I saw it.

The individual pictures were all a part of a whole, larger image. Each one, a glimpse into an imaginary window that overlooks a beautiful, picturesque field of wildflowers. Each "pane" was a different season.

"Amazing. Just amazing." I said, half to myself as much as to Trevor.

"Thanks, Dad. It means a lot." Trevor replied, almost as sheepishly as I had.

"Well, let's go get that Alfredo! And you're buying!" I said.

"Wait a minute! Why do I have to pay?" Trevor said, surprised.

"Well, you're the successful artist! You should treat your old man." I replied. Trevor just laughed, and we headed off to gorge ourselves on pasta.

*****

When we got to Alfredo's, they seated us pretty quickly, so we took to examining the menus as soon as we sat down. We were both starving and, frankly, couldn't wait to bury our faces in plates piled high with delicious, creamy pasta. I was salivating at the thought of the garlic knots they brought. To the table every time you came in. The giant bowl of salad they always bring out for the table made for a welcome sight for two hungry Gulley men.

I started filling my bowl before the server could even let go of the bowl.

"Soup?" the young man asked. I thought about it, and after only the slightest hesitation, agreed to a bowl.

I didn't even bother to ask what kind of soup was being served. All I knew was that I had a hollow leg that needed filling.

*****

After returning from lunch with Trevor, I found myself still determined to dig up some sort of evidence that Tuttle could use to crack this case. The Bösendorfer had to be somewhere, and I was going to find it.

A quick search online found the number soon enough. I called the moving company Sun and Moon Movers. They were the only ones who were open 24 hours, and it just made sense to start there.

I called the number I found on my phone using the maps application and immediately sent me to a voicemail system.

"Thank you for calling Sun and Moon Movers. We are away from the phone or on a job, moving customers' belongings with care and precision. If we can help you with the same care and precision, please leave a message after the tone."

Beep.

"Hey, this is Jack Gulley. I'm working on finding some information about a piano that was moved the other night from Devon Hall at the University. If anyone that was on that crew could call me back, I'd really appreciate anything they could tell me. Thanks!" My message was confident and direct. In reality, I didn't know if this was for sure the right movers, but it was a hunch. And, as far as hunches go, I was pretty confident in this one.

Since I was going to have to wait to see if I had hit pay dirt, I spent a little more time cleaning in my shop. I had been gone more than usual lately, and the assorted mail and papers lying around the counter was a testament to that.

I started by picking up a wastebasket. The next step was going to be to clean off the counter, and then the rest of the shop.

Ready. Set. Go.

CHAPTER EIGHT

THE SHOP LOOKED much better after about a half hour of cleaning while my favorite AC/DC was blasting over the speakers in the corner.

After settling back into my chair, I noticed I had voicemail on the store phone. I played back the messages.

The first message was from the moving company. More precisely, one mover that was on duty that night.

"Mr. Gulley. This is Mike Sorenson. I work with Sun and Moon Movers, the moving company? Anyway, they said you wanted me to call you. Listen, I'm about to go out on a call, but I can tell you that, yes, we moved a piano over at the University. I can't really tell you where. I understand you might be helping the police. Just have them call me. I'll gladly make a statement. I just don't want to do something wrong and get myself in trouble by telling my information to someone who's not a real cop before I tell the police, you know? I noticed the voicemail message said this was a music store. Thanks!"

Fantastic! You could've knocked me over with a feather. I called Tuttle's cell to give him Sorenson's information. My excitement to have found this clue was almost enough to take the sting out of the point Sorenson made about this being a music store and me not being a "real cop".

"Tuttle! I got some info that might help you. I got a message back from a Mike Sorenson of Sun and Moon Movers. He said they moved the piano the other night. I think he's going to call you, or the police, rather. Anyway, I hope it helps!" I said.

"Jack, I had a guy here at the station working on this already, and somehow you smoked him. You have good instincts. I'll get on this right away. Thanks!" Tuttle said.

I have to admit; I felt like this was just some kind of dream. Like the whole thing was going to fall apart around me. Then I realized; we may be closing in on the piano, but we still have absolutely no idea who had it moved.

No. Let me rephrase that. I had no idea who had it moved. Tuttle would have that information shortly after talking with the moving company. I just have to wait my turn to find out. Nail-biter anyone?

There was another message on the machine.

"Uh, Mr. Gulley? Uh, this is Todd Monday, Dr. Clark's assistant? You may not have heard of me, or maybe you have. Either way, I had some information that I thought you might want to pass on to Detective Tuttle? I mean, I know you're not a cop or anything? But I've been to your store. I play drums. Anyway, I knew how to get a hold of you, and I figured you could get a hold of him, so... Like I said, I have some information. Call me."

After hearing the message, I felt like I had found a new mystery to solve. The mystery of figuring out what the heck this kid was trying to say!

At any rate, I picked up the phone and looked at the caller ID. I hit dial under the number and waited as it rang.

"Um, hello?" I heard the familiar voice of Todd Monday on the other end.

"Hello. Todd? This is Jack Gulley. I got your message. What did you want to tell us, eh, I mean, what did you want me to tell Tuttle?"

"Oh, uh, sure. The thing I was calling you about was about Dr. Clark. I mean, I think it's about Dr. Clark..." Todd said, sounding very spacey.

"Maybe you could just give me the Cliff's Notes and I'll let Tuttle know what you said?" I offered as an out.

"Well, OK. So, what I was going to say was that Dr. Clark was probably the one who stole the piano." Todd said with an almost "nana-nana-boo-boo," tone to his voice, like a child who proudly

43

just told on another kid.

"Er, uh, OK..." I said." What makes you say that?"

"Well, how do I put this? I noticed the other day that Dr. Clark had been talking to the president. Of the University? Not of the country. You know? Anyway, so, like, I kind of overheard the conversation, and it wasn't a good one. I could hear Dr. Clark raising her voice and saying stuff about how people need the music program. I think they're thinking about cutting the music program. Now my thought is that she stole the piano and sold it so that she could have the money to run the music program herself." Todd said, sounding as if he were a proud poppa, announcing the birth of his first child.

I had only known of Todd for about 10 minutes, and already he had me worried. Both about the state of public education, and Todd's ability to dress himself.

"Now, Todd, I know Dr. Clark might be a little, well, out there, but do you really think she would have a priceless piano stolen just so that she could keep her job? Especially when you think about the fact that the very loss of the piano could jeopardize her job and the very music program itself?" I asked. "Besides, I think there was a moving company involved with transporting the piano, and Dr. Clark would never use a regular moving company to move the Bösendorfer. She wouldn't risk damaging it."

There was a long period of silence on the other end, and then he spoke up again.

"I hate her." Todd said.

"Er, what?" I asked. "Did you say "I hate her"?"

"Yes! She's awful!" Todd said. His voice was almost weepy now. "She's the worst person in the world! A monster!"

Now, I'll admit, Dr. Clark seemed like she could be, oh, how would you put it? Challenging? With that being said, one does not achieve their Ph.D., become the head of a department at a university, and, in most outward ways, achieve success by being "the worst person in the world" and "a monster".

"And exactly what am I supposed to do with this information?" I asked Todd. He seemed to take a contemplative pause.

"Take it to the detective. So he can arrest her." Todd said, almost seething now.

"I'll be honest with you Todd, I don't think that this information will hold water enough for detective Tuttle to arrest Dr. Clark." I told him.

"Fine! Never mind! I'll take care of it myself." Todd said in a huff.

Todd hung up the phone. And rather than just standing there in my store, holding a phone to my ear with no one on the other end, I did the same. As I hung up the phone, I wondered to myself about what exactly Todd meant by taking care of it himself. I was afraid that I knew. But could Todd be violent? I wasn't sure. It didn't seem like him, but it wasn't out of the realm of possibilities.

While Dr. Clark is a hard woman to like, I certainly wouldn't want anything bad to happen to her. I knew I should let Tuttle know what Todd said immediately. I picked up the phone and dialed Tuttle's cell. He didn't answer, but I left a message for him. I didn't feel much better about the situation, so I decided to go to the university and see Todd face-to-face and see exactly what he meant by what he said. I grabbed my jacket and headed out the door of the shop.

I fumbled for my keys while I half speed walked, half ran to my car. I dropped the keys while fumbling to unlock the car. I fumbled with the keys again, trying to put the keys in the ignition.

I was probably in no mental situation to drive. I may have been better off just staying at home.

After closing my eyes and taking a breath, I realized that if I didn't take a beat, I was going to most likely crash my car and not be of much help to anyone.

After I had re-centered, I started the car and somehow managed to drive to the University without incident.

CHAPTER NINE

BY THE TIME I made it to the University I was almost in a panic. I had been imagining all sorts of terrible things happening in my head on the way over, and I was just trying to decide which scene I would walk in on.

When I pulled into the parking lot, I parked my car illegally, jumped out, and ran to the rear entrance that was closest to the parking lot. I don't think I even closed my car door. The locked door just rattled as I pulled at the handle! I ran around the short brick wall with decorative bushes along the top, the branches and leaves scratching me as a brushed by them, and up the hill to the front of the building. I could already hear raised voices. What was Todd doing?!?

The front doors were open. Some luck, at last!

As soon as I headed up the stairs in the front lobby, the scream coming from the offices on the next level stopped me in my tracks.

"TODD!!!"

"What just happened!?!?" I thought or said aloud. I'm not even sure myself anymore! I sprinted up the rest of the stairs and down the hall to Clark's office and, channeling my inner Chuck Norris, kicked in the door with a crash, splintering the door frame, and what felt like my foot.

Dr. Clark shrieked and jumped back from the desk she was standing behind. "What in the heck do you think you're doing?!?" Dr. Clark said loudly, her look of shock and appall speaking volumes, not of whatever Todd had been saying, but of how she felt about me and my intrusion.

Todd was still sitting in the chair across the desk from Dr.

Clark, an aghast look on his face. His eyes were as wide as tennis balls.

"Wait! Todd!? You didn't hurt Dr. Clark?" I said, trying to catch my breath.

"Hurt me?? I knew you were up to something, you little pimple!" Dr. Clark said, her eyes narrowing as she focused her rage back on Todd. Todd just looked back at me with a hurt look on his face, like he couldn't believe I had broken some imaginary trust.

"I would not hurt her! Why would you say that?" Todd said.

Dr. Clark screamed vulgar and demeaning commentary at Todd that is best left out of this account.

Todd looked beaten down, defeated, as Clark spewed her venomous assault on his character and very being.

Something in Todd snapped. He raised his head and looked straight at Clark; he stood up out of his chair, seeming to fill with rage, like a balloon quickly filled with air, towering over Clark at his full height. Todd screamed at her with fire in his eyes and rage in his voice. "I HATE YOU! YOU CRAZY, EVIL CREATURE! I WISH YOU WERE DEAD!!" He was ranting like a lunatic on a street corner, warning all that the end of time was nigh.

He then picked up the chair he had been sitting in when I burst into the room and hefted it over his right shoulder and threw it straight at Clark, who dodged just in time. The chair smashed into the wall behind her, shattering her framed Ph.D. And leaving it dangling from the nail on one corner of the frame, glass shards peppering the floor.

Todd stormed out of Clark's office and down the hall. As Dr. Clark stood from her hiding place behind her desk, I asked her, "Are you alright?"

"GET OUT!!" Her eyes reflected the rage her mouth spewed forth.

I left. My foot was pounding all the way to my head now.

After I made it back to the front of the building, I heard Dr. Clark scream again, but this time I recognized it for what it was; a scream of rage. She had been screaming *at* Todd, not because of him.

I felt awful for assuming the worst of Todd, but after he flipped just then and threw that chair at her, I felt like my fears may not have been far off point. One thing I was certain of, Todd probably has one heck of a right hook. The way he threw that chair let me know I never wanted him to slug me.

I looked around me but didn't see where Todd may have gone. He was out there somewhere, though. And he was angry. I can't say I blamed him, but I just wished I could talk to him and make sure he wasn't planning to do anything stupid.

I thought that maybe *I* had done something stupid by just getting involved. I know Tuttle would prefer that I simply stayed out of this complete mess, but there was something about the thrill of finding out who the thief was and firmly sticking my nose squarely where it didn't belong.

Where I belonged, and where I hadn't been enough lately, was back at my store. While I'm sure the Bonaroo promoters hadn't made me the official supplier of musical instrument for all acts in their festival, I may have missed out on a couple of sales, regardless. Something was going to have to give. If I was going to be gallivanting around looking for clues as to what happened to the piano, I realized I may have to hire an employee to man my shop, at least part-time.

And while it looked like Todd needed a job now, I didn't think that he was quite who I was looking for. A vision of Todd throwing a Stratocaster across the room at a grumpy customer passed through my mind.

Nope.

A potential lawsuit and destroyed equipment is not in the job description I was dreaming up in my head.

Regardless of that, I needed to find a warm body to fill the seat behind the counter sometimes, regardless of my new hobby. I had been running things by myself for too long, and I was feeling the effects of burning the candle at both ends. Speaking of burning, my foot was about to pound out of my shoe at this point. I got out a Goody's headache powder to swish down and try to ease the throbbing pain in my foot. I was sure no bones were broken, but Jiminy Cripes, it hurt!

I decided to start simply.

I went to the local newspaper's website and within minutes I had written and paid for a classified ad that would bring me a few applicants for a clerk position at my shop. Or, at least, I hoped it would. Do people even read newspapers anymore? Time would tell.

I was looking forward to seeing who all would apply!

I called the newspaper's classifieds office, as I didn't think I could get the best deal by purchasing my ad through the website. It helps when you know the editor personally.

Geoff Mashburn was an old childhood friend who lived up the road from me and my family when we were young. He had gone on to college on a literary scholarship, which led him to majoring in journalism. When he moved back to Harrows Gate, he naturally became a reporter for the local newspaper. One thing led to another, and as you probably assumed, he eventually became the editor.

"Well, if it isn't the music man!" Geoff said as I entered his small office. "What's up, Jack?"

"I haven't darkened your doorway in a while, and I figured you were due." I kidded.

"You know you can darken my door anytime, brother! Where have you been hiding? I came by the store the other day and Sheila said you were out. How `ya plan on making a living that way, huh?" He said as he grabbed my hand in a firm handshake then gestured for me to take a seat.

"Well, I've been helping the police with an investigation. The grand piano I helped the University get? Someone stole it the other night. They asked me to come on as an advisor."

"Exciting!"

"Yeah, I have to admit, I've really been enjoying the investigation, and working with the detective assigned to the case. Even though I may cause more trouble than I'm worth to him." I chuckled nervously, thinking about busting into Clark's office like I did. That one is going to come back on me. I can feel it.

Geoff raised an eyebrow. Even though he was the editor of the paper now, I could see that journalist inside him getting curious.

"Anyway, we don't have much right now. I guess I'm just excited because it's all so new to me," I said. Geoff backed into his chair, seemingly backing off, for now at least.

"So, what brings you in, Jack?" Geoff asked, getting right down to business, as he was prone to do.

"I need to place a classified ad. I'm going to hire some help for the shop. Like you said, I was closed in the middle of the day. Can't do that right on, so I suppose I need to get somebody to be there when I can't. Also, I need to take a break sometimes, too," I said.

"Jack, if you'll forgive me, I remember before Michelle died. You guys were open when you were open and closed when it was your time together. You seemed to have a plan. After she was gone, I'll admit, it seemed like you just absorbed into that shop. You were there all the time. Don't think I didn't notice. I figured you were just coping in your own way. Throwing yourself into your work or something like that. I think getting out a little, even with the police officer…"

"Detective." I corrected.

"… detective…. whatever, is probably a good thing." Geoff looked a little like he was waiting for me to snap back that he was wrong, that he was reading too much into it all, but I didn't. I knew his journalistic intuition was as sharp as ever. He was right.

"Well, help me then. Let's put together a great ad so I can get some help for the shop," I said.

Geoff just smiled and pulled out his laptop.

My little ad would run in the paper later that week, even though I hadn't even come up with any interview questions yet. I was thinking about what creative ways I could glean the information

I would need to hire the right type of person I'd want to represent my store when I realized I had better get in front of the incident at Clark's office. I don't think she would give a flattering account of what happened when I showed up to Tuttle if she spoke to him.

I called Tuttle's cell, and it went to voicemail.

"Hey, Tuttle. So, I wanted to call and tell you about something that happened today. There was a thing. At Clark's office. I sort of got the wrong idea about Todd Monday and went to talk to them about it. Call me back and I can explain more. Thanks."

I hit the red X on my phone and sent that brief message into the ether. Now I was mercy to the fates. I made a little cross symbol like I was Catholic, even though I'm not. I just knew I needed God on my side now, because I might get to meet Him in person soon if Tuttle found out I busted into Clark's office and everything that transpired without getting to at least give my side of the story as my last words.

Tuttle is a great guy, but he can sure be intimidating.

Trying to put all that aside for the moment, I decided it was time to grab some lunch. My stomach was in some state between being tied in a knot and also wanting cheesy bread. I stopped in at Little Caesars Pizza for some grub. They had the cheesy bread, too. My mind was slowly drifting from the day's events to the garlic and butter and cheese trifecta that was gradually overtaking my consciousness.

I ordered and paid for my lunch combo and the cheesy bread, then turned on some music on my phone that was coming through my earbuds, then settled into a booth to enjoy the goodness that lay before me. The smell was divine. Maybe it wasn't a pizza parlor purists cup of tea, but I was always a simple guy when it came to food. I like a $5 pizza just as well as one I pay $30 for. If I can save a few bucks, I'm going to do it!

I sipped my Mountain Dew and grabbed a slice of my lunch special. The cheese stretched as I pulled the slice away from the box. The sauce smelled delicious. I was salivating at the pepperoni and sausage. Then I took the first bite.

Daniel Dykes

Heaven.

CHAPTER TEN

DETECTIVE TUTTLE WAS driving his 1987 Caddie to meet with Mike Sorenson of Sun and Moon Movers to see about getting some information about the piano. Jack had really come through with this. "Maybe that music-geek mind of his isn't so useless after all!" he thought, scratching the stubble on his neck.

The highway was empty this morning; the sun was shining, and Tuttle felt good about where this case was heading. Just a little information from the Sorenson guy, and he'd almost have this case wrapped up. It's exciting when things come together. It makes up for all the things you can't control from day to day. Life things.

As he drove, Tuttle couldn't help but let his thoughts wander. Specifically, he thought about his daughter. He missed her. He hadn't seen Jamie since the divorce, and Tuttle had only spoken to her a few of times since then. In the beginning, they kept in touch, but Jamie, as teenagers are prone to do, stopped calling as much, and coming by had almost completely dried up. He hadn't stopped thinking about her, though. He loved her more than anything. Certainly more than himself.

Tuttle was coming up on the exit and flipped on his turn signal. The clicking sound that the turn signal made was old-school, almost rustic by today's standards. He remembered being in a loaner car recently while the Caddie was in the shop. The turn signal made a clicking sound that came from the speakers. *The speakers!* Had we *really* come to that? Had we started going down *that* road? When even the click of a turn signal was synthetic? It seemed like everything was fake these days. People, things, beliefs... Tuttle didn't know if he could believe in anything anymore. Wasn't sure he wanted to. After all, he'd been let down so many times.

He had given up on love years ago after his divorce. He tried dating once or twice, but it never seemed right. He also realized that it all seemed forced. He was a loner. And not in a sad or angry way. Tuttle just thrived as a loner. He valued his freedom, and with his job being what it was, it was probably for the best. The only woman in his life was his daughter.

Tuttle could see the Sun and Moon Moving Company building up ahead, just past the red light on the left. As he pulled in, the Caddy creaked and rocked into the parking space right in front of the door. Tuttle unhooked his seatbelt, opened the heavy door to the Caddie, and stepped out and straightened his tie.

Tuttle knocked lightly, wondered to himself why he was knocking on the door to a business establishment that was open to the public, then opened the door to the moving agency and stuck his head inside.

"Hello? Detective Mark Tuttle, HGPD."

Nothing.

He moved inside and stepped up to the desk. It seemed like the room was contracting, Tuttle thought, but then he realized it was mostly because of the low ceilings. The walls seemed grimy and worn. Even after seeing someone had obviously repainted the walls multiple times, it still looked like they needed painting again. The floors creaked under his feet. It was a musty smell to the room that he attributed to an aging building. The front desk was essentially just an opening in the wall. There were some clear acrylic pamphlet displays, but only one had a single pamphlet that appeared faded and worn. Looking around the room, he noticed the general disrepair of the chairs that lined the walls for customers.

Tuttle heard an abrupt rubbing sound, like the noise made by someone opening a door that was out of alignment in its frame. A rather large man with a belly that hung well over his pants came out of a door that was on the wall behind the desk.

"May I help you?" the robust man asked Tuttle with an almost suspicious look on his face.

Tuttle started thinking about the way other customers must feel if they get that same suspicious look from him. Heck, he wondered if he gave the same look to people when he was interviewing witnesses for clues.

"Yes! I'm Detective Mark Tuttle, HGPD? I was told by Jack Gulley that he had spoken with a Mike Sorenson. I believe he's an employee here?" Tuttle said.

The guy with the belly looked at Tuttle's badge, which he was holding out for inspection to the man, and sat back into his chair behind the desk. The fat man picked up the phone on the desk and pulled at the cord a little to get some slack, then sat the phone base back on the desk on top of a pile of random papers. After a quick scratch of the afore mentioned belly, the man pressed one of the quick dial buttons and held the receiver to his ear. "Mike? There's a police officer here for you. What? No, I don't think so. Just come out here!" he said into the phone, then hung up.

A moment later, Mike Sorenson, a tall, lean man, stepped out of the door behind the desk and locked his eyes on Tuttle. He asked, "You needed to see me? Is this about the piano?"

"Actually, yes. It is. It is about the piano." Tuttle said. He was sure his eyebrows must have raised and his eyes widen.

"Oh, yeah. Just let me get my jacket." Mike said as he reached around the corner of the door to the office and pulled his jacket off of a hook that was hidden from Tuttle's view.

When they got outside, they stopped by Tuttle's car. "So, what have you got for me?" Tuttle asked Mike.

"So, like I told Mr. Gulley, we moved the piano from the University the other night. I didn't tell him much else because he wasn't a cop and I didn't want to do something wrong." Mike said.

"Can you tell me who it was who hired you?" Tuttle asked.

"No, actually. We got the call about 30 minutes before we showed up. The person who called just gave us an address. We showed up and there was a note on the door. It just said it was unlocked and gave us instructions to load the piano and where to take it." Mike said.

"If you never saw the person who hired you, how did you get paid?" Tuttle asked.

"There was an envelope with cash in it. It was sitting on top of the piano. We don't take checks anymore due to so much fraud. Most people pre-pay with a credit card. But we take cash, and generally speaking, we're happy to do it." Mike said.

"Didn't you think it was strange that there was nobody there when you went to move a really expensive, grand piano?" Tuttle asked with a tone that must have made Mike feel like he was being grilled. Mike squirmed a little.

"Er, uh, well, we were just there to do the job. She just wanted the piano taken to the address she gave us." Mike said, somewhat remorsefully.

"She?" Tuttle stopped him, "You said she. Was it a woman who hired you?"

"Well, yeah. I guess. All I know is the person on the phone that gave us the initial call was female." Mike said. "After that, we never really heard from anyone else."

"OK, here's the important part: *where did they have you take the piano*?" Tuttle asked with emphasis.

"Yeah, I figured you'd want to know that, so I got the note out of the truck. The one that was on top of the piano? It had the gate code and container number on the note." Mike pulled the crumpled piece of paper out of his jacket pocket and handed it to Tuttle.

Tuttle took the note and looked at it. No need to bag it for prints. The prints on the paper would probably all belong to Mike and the rest of the moving crew by now. No, he was more interested in seeing if the piano was still there. Tuttle pulled out his phone and called it into the department.

After getting a search warrant and contacting the owner of the storage facility, Detective Tuttle, Officer Garrison, and a couple of guys from forensics and a few other uniformed officers that were already patrolling the area convened in front of the storage unit. It was a metal building, built with corrugated metal sides and a sliding door made of the same material. It was an electronic lock on the door. Garrison punched in the code that was on the note left on the piano. The little light at the top of the pad went from red to green. Garrison took the handle to the door and slid it open. As light from the streetlights outside slinked into the building through the door, a beam cast upon what was obviously a large, grand piano under a tarp.

Tuttle smiled despite himself.

"Hold on. I want Gulley to look at this thing and make sure it isn't damaged. Start taping off the area and get ready to celebrate a closed case." Tuttle told Garrison.

"Absolutely!" Garrison said, and stepped off to fulfill his orders.

Tuttle knew it was late, but called Jack anyway.

CHAPTER ELEVEN

AFTER I GOT back to my car, I was waiting for the inevitable. And it happened. My phone began buzzing and when I looked at the screen, I saw the name of Tuttle glaring at me.

I reluctantly swiped my finger across the screen and held it to my ear.

"Hello, Tuttle." I said.

"Jack, I was going through my messages and I got yours. Something about Clark's assistant?" Tuttle said. I was trying to remember exactly what I had said in the message, but it wouldn't come to me. I was panicking!

"Uh, I really don't recall what I was going on about. Heh! You know me!" I stammered on. "So, busy day?"

"Well, yeah. I guess you could say that." Tuttle said, making me feel a little less like heading to Canada.

"So Jack, getting back to Mr. Monday. What was that all about? Did he tell you something pertinent to the case?" It felt like Tuttle was prying... or, more likely, I was just being delusional. Either way, I had to get out of that conversation for the time being, at least until I had a chance to see what he knew about what had just happened.

"Oh, not sure yet. Say, Tuttle, mind if I call you back? It's just I'm driving..." I replied, trying to find a way out of this conversation.

"Oh, okay. I'll let you go. Just get back with me if anything comes to you about your talk with Mr. Monday." Tuttle said.

He hadn't heard! He didn't know about the craziness that ensued in Clark's office! Somehow I had imagined Tuttle coming up behind me on the highway, with his light on the dash flashing, pulling me over and beating me with an old-fashioned police baton. I was glad I had dodged the bullet. The only problem I had now was that there may still be bullets flying.

I spent the rest of the afternoon and evening at the shop, coming up with questions for the interviews I would have to find some part-time help for the store. Rang up a sale on a bass guitar and rig for one of the old geezers in town. There was no doubt, by the looks of him, that he was wanting to feed his passion for bluegrass music. Just had a look.

That was what I loved about music. It knew no age limitations. Kids, their parents, and even their grandparents could all get the itch. And scratching that particular itch didn't mean hurting anyone. Instead, it could bring something beautiful into the world. A world that desperately needed beauty.

I really didn't want to think about what I had now termed "The Clark Incident". What happened in Dr. Clark's office was definitely a dark cloud hanging over me. I felt like this whole debacle never would've happened if I had just kept my nose out of other people's business. I hoped that Detective Tuttle never caught wind of this little outing, afraid that if he found out, I'd get grounded, or worse, he'd cut me out completely. I was too involved for that to happen now. I wanted to see this through to the end.

Later that evening, I was watching a little television and trying to relax and get the complete fiasco that happened at Clark's office out of my head.

I got up from the couch in my living room where I'd been sitting and walked down the hall to the bathroom and flipped on the light switch. I turned on the water at the sink and splashed some cold water on my face before looking up at myself in the mirror. My first thought was that I should apologize to Todd. If I hadn't come bursting into Clark's office like that, maybe none of this would've happened.

I reached for a towel and dried my face-off. As I walked out of the bathroom and flipped the switch back off, it occurred to me

I'd probably have to pay for Dr. Clark's door.

My fists clenched and my face winced as I groaned. All I wanted was just for this day to be over. I turned the corner and went into my bedroom, where I plopped myself onto the mattress and spread out my arms and legs. I laid there in the darkness and waited for sleep to take me, and I was almost there, too, and then the phone rang. Again.

CHAPTER TWELVE

IT WAS TUTTLE again. I was just about to drift off to sleep when the nightmares had come calling a little too soon. I knew it was too good to be true. He had found out about what happened at Clark's office and now I was going to hear all about how I had no business going out there, and I was no cop, and... well, here's where the party ends. Might as well just answer and let the onslaught begin.

I answered the phone but said nothing initially.

"Jack. It's me, Tuttle. You up?"

"Yeah, I'm up. Listen, I can explain..." I said without thinking.

"So, you're probably wondering why I'm calling so late. We found the piano. Or at least we think we did. At least this is the address that Sorenson gave me. I was wondering if you could come down and identify it?" Tuttle said.

I sprang up out of the bed. They'd found the Bösendorfer? It didn't seem real! I had forgotten all about Tuttle talking to Sorenson. Then the dizziness set in. Sat up too fast. I flopped back onto the bed and continued my call with Tuttle.

"Of course! Where do I go?" I said, wiping the sleep from my eyes.

Tuttle sounded happy. "Let me give you the address..."

The address that Tuttle gave me was at an old, abandoned tobacco warehouse. Tobacco farmers had stopped using these warehouses years ago, and they had since been purchased for use as an indoor flea market. It had nice, smooth paved floors and good lighting overhead. The walls and ceiling were all corrugated metal. There were two large corrugated metal sliding panel doors. They had already taped the area off with crime scene tape, looking like a scene from CSI. I saw Tuttle waiting for me by his car.

The air was crisp and cool, my breath visible in the lights of the squad cars. As I got out of my vehicle, I saw Tuttle notice me. He waved me over, and I went. To be honest, I was still waiting for the other shoe to drop. I knew that what happened at the University would most likely blow up in my face. It was just a matter of when?

The lights from the squad cars were blinding. Add the flashlights to be brandished by the uniformed officers as well, and it was almost dizzying.

"Are you throwing a rave out here?" I asked Tuttle, attempting to be droll.

"Hardly. Come on Jack, I need you to identify the body, per se," Tuttle said, being much more droll than I.

Touché.

As he held the tape up for me to step under, I glimpsed the piano inside the building. I immediately saw something that made me cringe.

"Well, it's obvious that the movers didn't have the right equipment to move the piano. Look at these marks left on the legs from where they used furniture straps," I said with regret in my voice.

"Well, I hate the piano took damage, but my job as a detective was to find it, not necessarily to find it in mint condition," Tuttle said.

And it was true. As amazing an instrument as the 290 was, Tuttle was right. The police couldn't be held responsible for the condition of a stolen item, even if it was a priceless, irreplaceable and incredibly beautiful piano. And this one was exquisite. There was a tarp laid over it, so I lifted the tarp back a bit from my position on the left side. I crept around to the front of the piano and raised the fallboard. The gorgeous keys were calling to me. I couldn't be faulted for testing the piano out, could I? Especially after it had gone missing. I, as the expert called in by the Harrow's Gate PD, *should* at least try it out, just to make sure it doesn't need any more repair. The truth was, I was beside myself to play this absolutely sexy musical instrument.

I positioned my hands for a magnificent C chord, and then I struck the keys.

Oh. No.

Nothing.

Like a dull thud.

"What did they do to you, you gorgeous thing?" I said to myself under my breath.

I moved swiftly around to the right side of the Bösendorfer and pulled the tarp the rest of the way off. I had originally thought that the lid was raised on the short lid prop, but had decided that the moving company had some sort of pad in the lid to keep it from bouncing. That wasn't the case. Something was in there. I lifted the lid of the piano.

Tuttle and a couple of uniformed officers had closed in behind me, watching intently as I raised the lid, waiting to see what the damage to the instrument was. A slight creak to the lid as I lifted it made us jump. We all realized just how silent the warehouse had become.

The silence got even more deafening. As I pushed up the lid without looking away from the scene inside the piano, it was Tuttle who broke the silence.

"Dr. Clark," Tuttle said in a hush.

Clark was laying face down inside the piano, her limbs in not quite natural positions, as if she had been hoisted up and thrown into the piano, her left arm laying awkwardly under her abdomen. Her coat had been thrown over her hurriedly. She had a red, black and blue mark on the right side of her face, and a large pump knot on her forehead.

"The killer may have been left-handed." Tuttle said.

"The blow to the right temple, right?" I asked, trying to get back to myself.

"Yeah." Tuttle agreed. "A lefty swings from their left side and would strike the right side of the face."

"And then Clark stumbled and hit her head." I presumed.

"That would be my guess. Good eye, Jack. We'll have to get the coroner to take a look to be sure." Tuttle said. He seemed a little impressed with my observation, especially since I'm an amateur sleuth.

Garrison came around to the back end of the piano, his flashlight in one hand, the piano lid prop in the other, gloved hand. "Detective? We may have the murder weapon here." Garrison held up the prop and showed it to Tuttle. There was blood and a few hairs wedged into the end of it.

"Yeah, looks that way. The blood and hair are most likely Clark's, but we'll need the coroner to sign off on that as well. Speaking of which, I'm going to call and see where Linda is. Wasn't expecting to need a coroner in a theft case. This just turned into a homicide case." Tuttle said, pulling his phone out and searching for his contacts.

Garrison continued to look around the area of the Bösendorfer. He was just about to give up when he stopped his flashlight on something on the ground, against the wall, behind the piano.

Garrison reached down with a gloved hand and picked up a fresh bottle of champagne. He bagged it.

"What's that?" I asked. "Looks like someone was getting ready to celebrate something, maybe?"

"Uh, before you get too far," I said to Tuttle, "I need to mention something. Let me tell you about my afternoon…"

CHAPTER THIRTEEN

ALL THINGS CONSIDERED, I would say Tuttle took my story about what happened in Dr. Clark's office pretty well. I mean, the shouting wasn't so bad, And I could hardly feel where he poked his finger in my chest anymore. I mean, I really couldn't feel it. It'd gone numb.

Apparently, they'll probably call me up as a witness in court. Todd, however, looks to be a prime suspect as the killer.

Tuttle had put me in his car because, as he put it, he "can't trust me to mind my own business". We were on our way back over to the University hoping to catch up with Todd. Tuttle wanted to meet Todd himself and slap some bracelets in front of his back, as the song goes.

I have to admit that Todd didn't seem like the type of person who could do this initially, but I had seen what I'd seen. My first impression of Todd was that he was just a whiny, stressed out young man that needed to get a different job. Of course, the explosive event that went down in Dr. Clark's office told me you never know what people are really like. Sometimes we see facades. The mask slips sometimes, though. Did Todd's mask slip? Is he really a monster? Or is there something more to this?

When we pulled up to the dorms, I set my foot out of the car, but Tuttle stopped me from exiting.

"Nope," he said, grabbing the sleeve of my jacket. "You stay here."

I just looked back like a scorned puppy as I pulled the door back shut with a slam. I looked out the windshield at the dorms. Tuttle just looked over at me and stared for a moment.

"Oh, for goodness' sake! Come on," Tuttle said.

I could feel the smile spread across my face like a kid on Christmas morning. In my upbeat mood, I hopped out of the car and slammed the door shut like a teenager. I clap my hands and rub them together and asked: "So what's our next step?"

Tuttle just looked square at me and said, "*MY* next step is to question Mr. Monday. *YOU* will remain silent and stay out of my way!"

"You got it!" I said. I was just happy to be along for the ride.

As we stepped up to the door, Tuttle being all detective-like, and me being more like an excited hype-man that was mute, we could see Todd peeking out the window already. We knocked on the door to Todd's room.

The door opened in a rush, Todd stepping into the doorway looking flustered.

"I'm really sorry. I really am. Wasn't myself… just so… upset." Todd was awkwardly forcing out the excuses. After we stepped into the room, we could see that Todd was packing. The room was a disaster, calculus textbooks lined the walls along the floor, math papers that, frankly, were beyond my comprehension, and other papers, papers everywhere. Papers with Dr. Clark's header on them. It looked like a hoarder house. There were also clothes that appeared to be wadded up and stuffed into the suitcase that was sitting open on the couch. Todd was about to run, it would seem.

Tuttle began reciting the Miranda Rights to Todd. I could see he was crying. Todd, not Tuttle. That surprised me. It hit me different. Not weeping, or sobbing, or anything, but he did. He cried.

CHAPTER FOURTEEN

LINDA RAINES, M.D. had been a medical examiner since she was 32 years old. Before that she had spent several years as a hospitalist, but she found that her preference was dealing with patients that were not able to walk and talk. Or breathe for that matter. She was 62 now and thinking about retiring soon. At least that's what she had been saying for a few years now. Her naturally white hair was kind of pretty in its own way, a result of being a fair-skinned redhead all her life. She found that the dungeon-like qualities of being an M.E. suited her complexion against the hostility of being in the sun very much.

Most people knew Linda for one thing that was not related to her ginger qualities. And she referred to them as qualities. "Never met a carrot top that wasn't the absolute best! Unless you count the actual Carrot Top. He's kinda annoying!" She would say.

It also had nothing to do with her skills as an M.E., though they were plentiful. No, it was none of these.

Linda Raines was a foremost connoisseur of coffee. No one could ever remember seeing her drinking anything else. People said she made agent Gibbs on NCIS look like a lightweight.

Tonight Linda had her best travel mug clenched tightly to her side as she watched the EMTs roll Dr. Clark's twisted body into her morgue.

"What have you got for me, boys?" she said aloud to the technicians as they carefully moved Dr. Clark's body over onto the table from the gurney.

"That's my vic, Dr. Brenda Clark, Ph.D.. Someone murdered her tonight." Tuttle stepped in from the double doors leading into the morgue. "What have *you* got for *me*, Linda?" He said with a sideways grin.

"Bring it in." Linda motioned to Tuttle, holding her arms out wide for a hug. Tuttle dropped his chin to his chest and laughed. He stepped forward, opening his arms in return, and the two embraced in a warm hug, like a mother hugging her son just in from college.

"You know I love to see ya, son, but you're always bringing in these deadbeats along with ya!" Linda made a broad, exaggerated gesture over her shoulder to the corpse of Dr. Clark.

"Linda! You're so tasteless!" Tuttle said with an expression like someone had just stomped on his toe.

"You gotta have a sense of humor down here in the hole," Linda said. *The Hole* was what the precinct lovingly termed the medical examiner's morgue and examination room. "You'll go nuttier than a bag of cats if you don't," Linda said with a look of someone who had just imparted a great nugget of wisdom.

"All right, let me see those crime scene photos. I need to see what I'm working with here," Linda said.

Tuttle handed over a folder full of pictures to Linda and she rifled through them, taking notes on a scrap piece of paper that was lying on the table next to her, while also taking a sip of her travel mug full of hot java.

"You know, Mark, I would much prefer you come down and visit me without also bringing some tragic end for someone to deal with when you do." Linda told him without looking up from the photos.

"If you don't like it, why don't you retire?" Tuttle said with faux hostility.

"You know? I just might, at that. Now is as good a time as ever!" She said as she put aside the photos and moved over to the cadaver of Dr. Clark.

Linda had been continuing her work while they talked. She had donned some rubber gloves and was currently probing her fingers all over the surface area of Dr. Clark's body. Finally, sitting down her coffee mug, Linda reached up and pulled down the lighted magnifying glass on an arm that extended from the ceiling and focused it on the side of Dr. Clark's head. Taking some forceps, Linda probed and poke at the tissue surrounding the wound on the side of Clark's head.

"Find anything interesting?" Tuttle asked.

"Not yet. Unless you count someone being murdered and stuffed inside a grand piano as interesting," Linda said, looking up at Tuttle through the magnifying glass, which made her right eye look gigantic to him. He couldn't help but chuckle.

Linda topped off her coffee mug and added a little powdered creamer and stirred them together.

"Now get out of here and let me work!" Linda said pointedly to Tuttle.

"OK, OK! I know when I'm not wanted," Tuttle said, raising his hands up in mock surrender.

Tuttle exited the examination room and headed back upstairs. Linda continued her examination of Dr. Clark by pulling the magnifying glass on its arm down to the body again, reaching to the table and grabbing her rather enormous mug of coffee and taking a sip.

"Mmm. Now that's what I'm talking about!" She said to herself.

CHAPTER FIFTEEN

WITH ONLY HAVING left Todd Monday's dorm room apartment a few hours earlier, the facts surrounding the events that led to Dr. Clark's murder were spinning in my head. To say I couldn't sleep was an understatement. Tossing and turning in my bed, I eventually just sat up on the side and stuck my feet out to stretch, rubbing my eyes as well. It was as if I had drank a pot of coffee just before bed.

The craziness of everything that had transpired was fascinating, and more than a little chilling. Todd was obviously a guy with issues, but then again, Dr. Clark would give anybody issues. She treated him unprofessionally, some would say even inhumanely. I can't say truthfully that I wouldn't lose it with her as well if I were in his position. People have committed murder for less than the way she treated him.

I pulled the covers over me as I rolled back into bed and turned to my side, tucking the sheet and blanket between my neck and shoulder. Stretching my legs out, feeling the cool sheets caress my feet, ankles, and calves, I closed my eyes and listened to the silence of my room. I could hear the rustle of the sheets as I tightened my grip on the blankets. Maybe I could sleep. But, no. The longer I laid there in the silence, the louder my thoughts got. I wasn't completely sure what those thoughts were yet, though. All I knew was that my mind was racing at a pace that would dizzy Mario Andretti. What? What was it? What was it my mind kept racing to figure out?

I threw the covers off and sat up on the side of the bed again. As my feet planted on the floor and my hands rubbed my eyes, I let out a deep sigh. This wasn't working. I needed sleep. I've been so busy chasing this little bit of adventure and intrigue in my life around that I hadn't fully realized how exhausted I was. And I was that exhausted. I had to get some sleep somehow.

I stepped down the hall and into the kitchen. I didn't bother flipping on a light. I had a small nightlight plugged into the wall above the sink for that. I opened the refrigerator and reached in for the milk. I got a glass down out of the white shaker cabinets. I set the glass on the stove and twisted the lid off of the jug of milk. As I poured the ice cold milk into the glass, I imagined Todd struggling to roll Dr. Clark into the piano.

The piano. How did the piano fit? Why would Todd move the piano, lure Dr. Clark to the storage facility, kill her and put her in the piano? It was almost comically absurd. I just couldn't wrap my head around it. I mean, in Dr. Clark's office, even though he showed outward hostility by throwing a chair at her, why would he go to all the trouble? But then again, the piano had to be stolen before the murder, obviously. Maybe there was no connection to the two crimes. Heck, as far as that goes, how do we know Todd even had anything to do with the piano going missing?

I looked down at my milk, picked it up, and took a swig. It needed something else, so I reached into the cabinet and pulled out a bottle, but hesitated at first. I knew what it meant if I took that lid off and started. I told myself I wouldn't. With a hint of shame welling inside me, I realized I was breaking that promise.

Could I live with myself?

I guess we'd have to see.

I twisted the lid and tilted the top into the glass. Not too much, just enough.

I'll admit, I poured a little more that I should have, but I didn't care anymore. I just wanted to get it across the tongue. I picked up the glass, swirled around, and tipped back the glass to my lips.

That's it. Just what I needed.

Chocolate milk is always the best!

It's funny how just adding one thing to something ordinary can make it extraordinary. All you have to do is add a little chocolate syrup to a regular glass of milk and, voilà! A delicious treat. But in the case of Dr. Clark, the thing that was added just makes it foul. If you look at the stolen piano, and all the clues surrounding it, by itself, it makes sense. If you look at the murder of Dr. Clark, in and of itself, it *almost* makes sense on its own merits as well. But when you put them together, something just doesn't quite add up!

As I couldn't sleep anyway, I decided to put pen to paper and try to figure out what we could've missed. I sat down on my couch, took a scratch piece of paper, and began to write down freehand everything I could think of dealing with this craziness. First of all, someone had stolen the piano. Check. I came across the program mentioning Autumn's concert. Check. The moving truck. Well, I got lucky there. If I hadn't remembered the dream I had, I never would've thought about checking on those moving companies. But I'll take it, subconscious assist and all! Check.

Let's see, I thought, *what about the storage facility?* Who had rented out the warehouse? No check here, but I'm sure Tuttle's looked into that, so I'll call him in the morning.

I couldn't help but feel like Autumn Baylor could know more about all of this. She was around Dr. Clark, and by virtue Todd Monday, all the time. Maybe she could tell us more about their… problems?

"… Nuh!" I grunted as I pulled my head up from my chest, apparently waking up from nodding off. I guess the deep thought had allowed me to slip into some sort of sleep after all. Now just to make it to bed.

I stood up from the couch. Ouch! My back is telling me I need a new couch. Or a new back, I can't tell. Either way, too expensive. I'll have to live with both for a while.

As I laid down and pulled my covers back over me, I dropped my foot out of the covers to the side of the bed. I've done this since I was a kid. I feel like it helps me regulate my temperature. Don't judge.

The sleep came quickly this time. I drifted off without even really realizing it. And I was just fine with that.

CHAPTER SIXTEEN

TUTTLE SAT AT his desk, covered in files of various investigations he had been assigned, some old and cold, some so fresh the ink still smelled hot.

A great big mess.

Tuttle sighed and started attempting to gain some semblance of order on the desk, stacking files, then arranging in alphabetical order. That was about as far as he could take it before he was at the threshold of his capacity for organization.

He pulled out the file on the Clark murder and flipped it open. He was looking over the evidence and remembered that the question of who rented the warehouse where the piano was found was still in the air.

Tuttle looked at the number in the file and picked up his desk phone and dialed.

After a few rings, the warehouse office picked up.

"Hello? Harrow's Gate Warehouse. Ron Winston." the man on the other end answered.

"Yeah, this is Detective Mark Tuttle with the Harrow's Gate Police Department. I'm calling about the warehouse space that you rent out for flea markets and the such over on Market Street? I need to know who rented that space last."

"We didn't. I'm glad you called, `cause I was jus' gonna' call you." Ron replied.

"Okay... what have you got?" Tuttle asked, his curiosity aroused.

"Okay, so after I found that piano, or whatever, out in my warehouse, I called you guys because, hey, it looked expensive. I thought there might be a reward... is there a reward?" Ron asked.

"Go on." Tuttle said.

"Okay. I had to ask. Anyway, after your people left with the piano, I had to lock back up. And at the time, I didn't think much of it, but the chain I lock the gate up with seemed off a little. Then today I was unlocking the gate, and the chain slipped out of my hands and fell off when I took the lock off. It just slid between the chain link and hit the ground." Ron said.

"When I went to pick up the chain, I saw it." He added.

"What did you see?" Tuttle asked, getting a little frustrated with Ron.

"Okay, I'm gettin' there! Calm down! It was a cut link." Ron said.

"A cut link of the chain?" Tuttle asked or exclaimed. He wasn't quite sure.

"Yes! I kept thinkin' the other night that the chain was off somehow. It was! It was shorter than I was used to. I been using that chain for years. I know exactly what link I've been hooking that pad lock through for as long as I've owned this place. Looked like somebody cut off the one link and locked back up to make it look like nobody had been through the gate." Ron said.

"Probably hoped it would buy time to get away after the murder. If someone saw the gate was unlocked, they may have called the police, and we'd be on their trail sooner." Tuttle said. "Have you touched the cut link?" He asked, saying a brief prayer in his head.

"Nope. Figured you boys would want to check for prints." Ron said.

Prayer answered! Tuttle thought. "Thank you!" He said.

"Leave it where it is and I'll be out to collect it soon."

*****

Tuttle drove the Caddie out to the warehouse site, with the forensics team following closely in a separate car, and was met by the owner at the gate. Ron was wearing coveralls that had the simple logo of the operation emblazoned on the back, and "Ron" in a red hand script on the left breast.

"So, where is this cut link?" Tuttle asked, stepping out of the car and slamming the door behind him. Tuttle knew he had missed a clue, and he was intent on finding it. He lived for justice, but he had to admit that he liked coming up with the smoking gun himself from time to time. At any rate, physical evidence is always a glorious thing to have, especially when a murder was involved.

"So, here's the chain," Ron said, presenting the scuffed and obviously aged chain, the lock still hanging from one link, "and over here's the little, cut off link." He said, pointing to the ground at his feet.

Tuttle pulled a pen from his pocket and hooked the small piece of chain link on it and slipped it into a small evidence bag.

"And what about the cut part of the fence? Have that here somewhere?" Tuttle said excitedly.

Ron pointed near the corner of the fence and nodded that direction as well. "Yup. Right there." Ron said, motioning over the general area where the corner of the fence was pulled back.

Tuttle left the fencing where it laid. He would have forensics photograph the area before collecting the individual pieces. *Seems sloppy,* he thought. If this was the doings of a driven person, methodical was not how anyone would describe how this little heist was planned. It looked like it was the work of someone who didn't know what they were really doing. But they stole a piano. Maybe they didn't intend to sell the piano. Then what was their intent? They just needed a cool casket for the victim of the murder they were about to commit? It didn't make sense, really. Unless the murder was the unexpected part. The piano was the only crime they planned to commit, and the murder of Clark was just for what? He didn't know yet.

Whoever it was who did this had tried to evade detection, but just barely. They didn't seem too worried about getting in here, with all the sloppiness, but the murder of Clark had to be a murder of convenience, didn't it? They usually plan premeditated murder better than this was. That's why it's called premeditated. This seemed almost like an accident being covered up, except Clark was dead, and it wasn't because she choked on a bite of spicy burrito. Linda said it was a blow to the head.

Forensics was getting their photos and following up on the work they had done the night before. Tuttle pulled his coat back and more prominently displayed his badge. He raised his hand up and motioned for the forensic photographer to come to the fence where the chain-link had been cut and pulled back.

"What've we got, Detective?" asked the forensics officer as he walked up to Tuttle.

"I wanted you guys to get some photos of this area around the fence before any of the stuff is picked up, and check for any other physical evidence in that area." Tuttle explained while reaching into his coat pocket and pulling out the link from the chain in it's little evidence bag. "I also want you to look this thing over and see if you get any prints." Tuttle handed the baggie with the link in it over to the other officer, who, after examining it through the bag, proceeded to place it into a small evidence container that they were using to collect all the bits of fence as well.

Tuttle reached for his phone and dialed the station. "This is Detective Tuttle. Transfer me to Raines."

After a moment, Linda Raines came on the line; "Raines here."

"Linda, I have forensics getting some evidence. Can you help with checking for prints? There's going to be a lot of small parts coming. They could probably use the help."

"Sure thing, honey. I can take care of whatever they need me to help with. Just remember, though, you owe me a pizza from that Rubio's place that Jack was talking about."

Tuttle chuckled. He'd buy everybody at the station pizza if they wrapped this case up in a bow.

"You got it! And maybe I'll throw in bread sticks, too!" He said.

"Don't tease me, Mark Tuttle." Linda warned in a faux stern voice.

"I would never!" Tuttle retorted.

CHAPTER SEVENTEEN

THE NEXT MORNING, I called Autumn Baylor and asked to meet her downtown for coffee. I had a few questions for her that might shed some light on the subject of the murder of Dr. Clark. I asked her if she might remember something that could've happened between Dr. Clark and Todd Monday. It took some convincing, but she agreed to meet with me. I guess college students can't pass up free coffee and pastries.

When I arrived at the café, I was quick to notice that Autumn had brought along her friend, gum girl. Gum girl looked a little reluctant to be there, a cool look on her face and plenty of product in her short blond hair. That, along with her completely blacked out sunglasses, and she seemed more like a rockstar on holiday than a college student. They were sitting at an outside table on the patio of the café, a broad, burgundy umbrella casting just a little shade overhead. The table was one of those ornate cast-iron types, better suited for decoration than actual dining, but I'm not one to criticize.

"Well, hello there Autumn and… Marissa?" I fished.

"Andrea. It's Andrea." The blond girl said with a look on her face like I was the biggest idiot she'd ever met. Of course! Why hadn't I read her mind like any normal person would have? But, hey, finally! A name for the face!

"Oh, I'm so sorry I never introduced you. When you talked to Andrea at the house, I just assumed… anyway, hello. So, what exactly was it you wanted to talk to me about?" Autumn said a little hurriedly.

"Well, actually, what I was curious about was the relationship between Todd Monday and Dr. Clark. I was wondering if you could shed a little light on that subject?" I asked her as I pulled a chair from another table set and turned around to face the table they were already sitting at. I sat down and waved my hand at the server. As the server stepped to the table, he brought a pot and topped off the coffee cup already on the table, and brought a full glass of soda to replace the one that was mostly drained. I was planning on treating the girls, but they apparently didn't want to wait and had ordered ahead of me.

"Is there anything I can get for you, sir?" The server said with a raised eyebrow and hopeful look.

"Let's see, I think I'll have the Americano with cream. No, wait. Let's make that a flat white." I said, hoping I didn't look like much of a coffee snob. I'm really not. I had just been to this particular café before and someone recommended the flat white once. I liked it, so...

"Oh, I'll be picking up the tab for the table." I mentioned. He just nodded and went to go get my coffee. "So, now that I've said that, what exactly did you order before I got here?" I said with a smile, hoping to get a chuckle. No such luck. Gum chew... er, Andrea sat staring, as cool as ever. Autumn, on the other hand, seemed somewhat distant.

When the server returned with my coffee, I picked up the cup and took a sip. Autumn just watched, her hands one laid over the other on the table. Andrea just sat, leaned back slightly, and stared.

"So, Autumn, I can understand how you might be shaken up over what happened, but I'm sure you knew Mr. Monday and Dr. Clark didn't have the best relationship. And that's what I was hoping to talk to you about. I thought maybe you could remember something about any of their interactions that might have given you a clue that Todd might be capable of something like this?" I asked.

"Yes." she said hesitantly. "Now that you mention it, I do remember Todd and Dr. Clark arguing. It was the night of my recital. The night the piano was stolen? I could see them off stage behind the curtains, arguing while I was playing. It seemed to be quite heated." Autumn said.

Andrea's eyebrow just cocked as she tilted her head slightly as if to say, *there you go, all settled*.

"Ever happen to find out what the argument was about?" I asked.

"No. I never really asked. I didn't want to pry. I figured it was their business and not mine." Autumn said contritely.

I turned to face Andrea, and pose the question to her. "What about you? Have you ever seen any strange goings-on?"

Andrea's only reply was to take her hands out of the arms crossed position they were in and cover her eyes, her ears, and her mouth in succession, making the fairly obvious see no evil, hear no evil, speak no evil. Autumn watched, rolled her eyes, and just looked down and off to the side. I didn't want to pretend to understand what was going on between those two, but they obviously had some sort of secondhand, unspoken communication.

A moment later, both girls got up, collected their things and gave their goodbyes. As they walked across the street towards Autumn's car, I noticed Autumn looking over her shoulder, as if she was afraid I would be right behind her, ready to ask more questions. I know Autumn must feel like I'm bothering her a lot, but I just want to see this through. Not sure why, it just feels important to me. As they both drove off in a rush, Andrea looked out the window at me with a grin on her face, and saluted with two fingers to her brow.

It felt more like a single finger to the sky, but I digress.

I went back to the table and paid the tab. One of the girls had a Diet Pepsi, and the other had a black coffee. I never noticed who was drinking what. I realized that I hadn't touched my flat white, so I took a sip and sat back in my seat. Something was eating at the back of my mind about the girls, but I couldn't put a finger on it yet. Something wasn't right, but I couldn't place it.

I thought about Todd and tried to wrap a bow on the whole affair, mentally at least.

It wasn't working. I still couldn't stop thinking about the

girls.

Not like that. Get your mind out of the gutter. I was mostly thinking about the look on Autumns face. And the flightless bird Andrea gestured me as they drove away. Something was off.

I left the cafe and went back to my place.

As I was driving home, I remembered that my intent was to call Tuttle this morning and see what he'd found out about the storage unit. I had completely forgotten in my eagerness to meet up with Autumn and gum girl. I fumbled around in the seat for my phone and hit Tuttle's number.

"This is Detective Tuttle. Hey, Jack." I heard after what seemed like less than a full ring.

"Hey, Tuttle. What, if anything, did you find out about the storage rental?" I asked.

"Not much more than what we already gathered. Monday signed the rental agreement from the storage company. The secretary at the storage company verified the slip." Tuttle said. "I scanned a copy of it with my cell phone. I'll send you a copy. You can see what I mean."

I got the scan of the rental agreement almost immediately. I scanned over the document and saw Todd's scrawl of a signature at the bottom, next to the initials of the secretary for the storage company.

"Jack, that's going to have to satisfy you now. I can't let you do any more amateur sleuthing on this case. I'll let you know when we have it all in the bag. Then you can celebrate the case closing, or whatever." Tuttle said.

It seemed like that wouldn't be long, too. It was looking like it was all going to be wrapped up nicely. Todd was looking more guilty with every passing breath.

*****

Back at the store, I had to get caught up on some repairs that were languishing on my workbench. A truss rod bent on a decent enough looking Stratocaster, so I replaced the neck and adjusted the tension before calling the customer to schedule a pickup. I soldered the wiring to a tone pot on a lovely Gibson Les Paul

Custom in order to eliminate a nasty crackling noise that was coming out of the amp whenever the knob was turned.

After I figured out that the reason the first valve of a trumpet was spinning freely and not locking into place was because of the kid having never added the first drop of valve oil to the horn, I oiled it, popped it back in, and sure enough, it went right into place. I called his mom and told her there would be no charge. After all, I didn't really *fix* anything.

I was tired, so I looked at the clock. It had only been an hour. Bleh. I spent the rest of the day planning a sale on strings, cables, and other accessories. Those kinds of sales did better than sales on instruments. People like to stock up on the little stuff when there's a sale. Picks and guitar polish go fast. Tuners sell like hotcakes!

After I finished up with my sales flyer in the computer, I looked at my watch again. This time I had spent a surprising amount of time on designing the flyer. Buried in the computer, I suppose. It was finally closing time. I closed out my register, and the till balanced, so I locked everything up and headed home.

That night I was beat. All this craziness and running the music shop had almost laid me out.

I had a small dinner and a hot shower, then crashed into my bed.

Sleep came quickly, for once.

CHAPTER EIGHTEEN

A FULL DAY had passed since his arrest, but Todd Monday was still as scared as he was from the moment they put the handcuffs on his wrists. The officer was holding him by the elbow, and the chains that bound the handcuffs and ankle cuffs in the middle seems slightly too short. With every step that Todd took his arms jerked down ever so slightly. It was just enough of an annoyance to take an already miserable and terrifying experience and make it aggravating as well. The officer stopped him at a yellow line at the end of the hall, just before the chain-link gates that open into another hall.

After the gates were opened, and authorizations passed, Todd was taken further down the hall and into a small 8 x 10 room. There was a table in the middle of the room and a stainless steel bench bolted to the floor. The investigator's two chairs were on the opposite side of the table. The suspects bench was bolted to the floor to prevent movement away from the camera's view, which was mounted in plain sight in the upper corner of the room. Todd noticed everything was built with a stainless steel finish. *Perhaps it makes it easy to clean up after an intense interrogation,* he thought in terror.

As Todd was cuffed to the desk and chair, he looked at the large, mirrored window and wondered who was on the other side.

A moment later, the door opened and Detective Mark Tuttle swiftly came into the room with a folder that he laid on the desk, and then sat down opposite Todd. Tuttle flipped open the folder and flipped around a picture from the crime scene of Dr. Clark in the piano. Todd looked at the photo and went silent, his face draining of all color.

"You recognize the person in the photo?" Tuttle asked.

"..."

"What are you thinking, Mr. Monday?" Tuttle was being friendly and calm, for now.

"..." Todd's mouth opened, but no sound was coming.

"Dr. Clark was your boss. How do you think this happened?" Tuttle asked, trying to give Todd an opening to explain, and maybe confess.

"I... I... I have no idea, but..." Todd said sheepishly, almost inaudibly.

Todd closed his fists together and pulled them into his lap. He never took his eyes off of the photo of Dr. Clark in the Bösendorfer. Tuttle waited patiently in silence, letting Todd fully take the image in, waiting for Todd to break that silence.

Todd slowly looked up at Tuttle with tears in his eyes.

"Do you think I did this?" he said in disbelief, followed by a sudden look of acknowledgment over his face, realizing that, yes, the detective *did* believe he did this.

"Didn't you?"

Todd silently and purposely looked back at the photo with a determined look on his face.

"*No!*" He shouted defiantly. Todd began pulling at the chains and rocking back and forth on the small steel bench.

Tuttle asked again, louder this time, and more pointed. "Did you do this? *Did you murder Dr. Brenda Clark?*"

"NO! I didn't do it!" Todd shot back at Tuttle, this time a bit more angry. He began jerking at the chains again, this time more focused, as if he were trying to break them.

"Just stop, Todd." Tuttle said, his tone returning to calm and collected. "You're not going to break those chains. You'll just hurt yourself."

"But I'm telling you, I didn't do it!" Todd declared.

"Well, if that's so, it will all wash out in the end. Until then, you can make yourself comfortable in your cell." Tuttle waved at the door for the officer just outside the interrogation room door, who nodded and stepped in. The officer unchained Todd from the desk and led him out of the room and back down the hall to his cell.

Todd sat in his cell silently, looking down at his feet. The generic version of Crocs that were issued to him squeezed a little as he turned his foot ever so slightly, drowned out by the screech of steel on steel that was followed by a loud slam of metal and the click of the the cell door being shut and locked. Todd sighed audibly and rolled onto his this mattress on the metal bunk, but didn't close his eyes. Sleep wouldn't be his tonight. No. Only the image of Dr. Clark's contorted body in that damn piano.

CHAPTER NINETEEN

TUTTLE SAT AT his desk, rolling a pencil back-and-forth over the papers that were scattered in front of him. He picked up his coffee mug and took a sip. Coffee helped him think. *Todd Monday is guilty as the day is long,* he thought. *He has to be.* The nagging in the back of his brain wouldn't stop pestering him, though. After sifting through some papers, Tuttle looked back through the file on the Bösendorfer/Clark murder case again. What was he missing? Something didn't add up. He had his man, Todd Monday. All signs pointed to Todd!

First of all, there's the piano, Tuttle thought. *Todd could have the piano removed, or rather stolen, in order to torture Dr. Clark and further increase the chances of her losing her program. Makes sense. But why go to all that trouble if you're just going to kill her? There's the little outburst Todd had in Clark's office that Jack told me about. It shows that Todd was angry enough with Dr. Clark to kill her, certainly. Maybe it was an act of passion? He went into another rage and killed her? No way to know, and he's not telling.*

"You're an angry man, Todd Monday." Tuttle said aloud.

Tuttle picked up his phone and dialed Linda Raines, M.E.

"Hey, sweetie. What's up?" Linda answered.

"Linda! Hey. I wanted to see if you'd come up with anything on the Clark case. Learn anything?"

"Hold on... let me get the file." Linda said, as the sound of the phone clunking down on her desk came over the line. "*And top off my coffee.*" Linda yelled from the other side of the room.

"Okay," Linda said, as she picked up the phone and adjusted it under her chin. "I have the file right here now. Subject Clark, Brenda, Ph.D.. Dadda-dadda-dadda... Okay, so basically the gal was struck upside the head with what I'd say is definitely the piano's lid prop. Just guessing from the residue that was left in the wound and the general look of the wound, shape of the impact site, etc.... Say, was the thing picked up by Garrison? His prints were all over it. You need to tell that boy how to properly handle evidence. That little.... Anyway, they only got a partial print, mostly because of Garrison screwing the pooch on the pickup of the probable *murder weapon. Ahem*. Let's see, crushing damage to the temporal and parietal bones of the skull were minimal for as far as a big, glorified stick to the head goes." A slurping sound came over the line as Linda sipped her coffee. "Alright, and as for the damage to the frontal bone of the skull and tissue, damage to the dermal layers, pretty insignificant. Seems like it was more likely to give her the idea for the Flux Capacitor than kill her." Raines quipped.

"Wait, are you saying that the victim didn't die from the blows to the head?" Tuttle asked, somewhat surprised.

"That is, indeed, what I'm saying." Linda replied.

"Well... what killed her?" Tuttle asked slowly.

"Asphyxiation." Linda replied.

"You mean they choked her to death?" Tuttle asked, a little flummoxed.

"Yeah, hon. It looks like after someone knocked her out, somebody made sure to finish the job." Linda made a loud slurp on her coffee and smacked her lips. "Seems like she was probably already out when the choking happened. Probably why you didn't notice it at the scene. She didn't put up a fight 'cause she was out cold."

"Jesus. This case is the weirdest thing I've investigated in the course of my career. Okay, thanks, Linda. I appreciate it." Tuttle said.

"Hang in there, sweets. You got this! I gotta get to lunch." Linda said quickly.

"Uh-huh. Grab a chili-cheeseburger for me, will ya? Leave it on my desk." Tuttle replied.

"Salad. Check. Boy, I'm going to get you to eat healthier if it's the last thing I do in this life. Bye, boy!" Linda said and hung up.

Tuttle rubbed his face and exhaled. He now had a premeditated murder. No chance this was a crime of passion. The killer had knocked out Clark and then, after she was already out, decided to finish the job.

Tuttle thought about how people can do things like this. Kill. How empty does someone have to be to take another person's life?

Those were questions he could ask Todd Monday. But Monday didn't seem like he was bright enough to pull this off on his own. Somebody had to have been helping him. Maybe it would be a good idea to go straight to the top and start putting some pressure there. The President of the University had to have something to say about her department chair being murdered. *Jack may have a connection there that could get us in.* Tuttle thought.

Jack's number was now on Tuttle's speed dial. Hesitantly, he tapped the screen. Tuttle heard the sound of the ring tone over the phone. Tuttle sighed and waited for Jack to answer.

"Tuttle! That you?" Jack's voice said over the line.

"Yeah, Jack..." Tuttle said. "I have a favor to ask."

CHAPTER TWENTY

TUTTLE AND I were just stepping into the door of Dr. Kinzel's office when we were approached by a smartly dressed young woman with blonde hair that was pulled tightly back and wearing thick-rimmed glasses. She was asking "who are you?", "what do you need?", "do you have an appointment?", etc. I was just about to stammer out something about whether I could set an appointment time when Tuttle flashed his badge in the girl's face and set his own appointment for "right now".

"I thought you were pulling some strings to get us in." Tuttle said, a little flustered. I just shrugged. When Tuttle called me last night, I was so excited to do some more sleuthing, I would have said I could fly if I thought it would get me back in the field. Besides, Tuttle was able to flash a badge and get in anywhere he needed. I wondered silently if there was a way I could figure out how to get into places *without* the use of a police badge.

However, at that moment, the badge was working marvelously. I was beginning to think making friends with a police detective would be a glorious thing for me. Imagine all the perks! Need into an exclusive club? Badge to the face! Want a better deal on a car? Badge to the face!

Was I thinking all of this out loud?

"Badge to the face!" Tuttle said sarcastically, while quite literally sticking his badge in my face.

Yikes. "Sorry." I said. Tuttle just put his badge back on his hip and shook his head.

"Gentlemen, what can I do for you?" a voice said. "I'm Dr. Marsha Kinzel. I'm the President here at H.G.U. Do you have any more information about Dr. Clark's case?" said one of the most exquisite women I'd ever met. She was no Michelle, but dang. Just dang. In a bookish sort of way. She had wavy brown hair, pouty lips, and legs that went all the way to her hips. I was a little smitten.

Please tell me I wasn't still thinking out loud! I looked around at everyone. If I was, no one seemed to notice, so I was clear.

"We still have Todd Monday in custody, Dr. Kinzel, and he is still our most likely suspect. But one thing he said was interesting. He mentioned that you and Dr. Clark had been heard arguing over something. He said he thought you might be thinking about shutting down the music program. Is this correct?" Tuttle asked.

"Ah, so that's it. Todd heard that, did he?" Kinzel said. She motioned us to her office. "Sarah, could you bring some coffee for the detectives?" she ordered her secretary.

"Oh! I'm not a detective. I'm a musician." I said.

Kinzel looked confused and turned to Tuttle. Tuttle didn't acknowledge and continued his point. "Mr. Monday also mentioned that Clark may have had the piano stolen to sell in order to pay for funding the music program." Tuttle said, half making a statement, but leaving it open for interpretation. A sort of verbal version of the way people like to make posts on Facebook and just say *I'm just going to leave this right here...*

"Well, I'm sure I have no idea about anything to do with that. What else did Monday say?" She asked.

"He told me a bit about how the good doctor was a maniacal, emasculating she-beast and a severe egomaniac." Tuttle said.

I was a little shocked. I had never heard Tuttle say anything like that. It seemed so unlike him, even if he was thinking it, I'd never imagine him saying it, but there it was. All I could think was "Wow"!

They both looked at me. Crap.

"Out loud again?" I asked.

"Yeah." Tuttle said.

"He also seemed very surprised by the sight of Clark being dead. You know, I had to wonder if that was all an act." He said.

"Really? You think he was pretending that he was surprised?" Kinzel asked with a softening of her voice, not quite a whisper, but noticeably softer, and leaning in like she was hearing a secret.

"It's possible. Sure." Tuttle said, matching her tone and posture.

"Surely not! I would stand by his credibility any day. I'm sure he couldn't kill someone." Kinzel said, looking a little saddened by the idea.

"Okay. Well, what about you?" Tuttle whispered. "Where were you the night Clark was killed?"

Kinzel's expression changed immediately. She suddenly realized what Tuttle was getting at. She straightened and her eyes looked to one side as she took a cooler demeanor.

"Tuttle, could I ask you something? In private?" I asked.

"No." Tuttle snapped.

"OK." I said, like a child being scolded by a parent.

"I have no idea what you're talking about. I was at home. You certainly don't think I did this, do you?" Kinzel said, seeming to get angry at Tuttle.

At that, they both stood, eyes locked. The tension was palpable. I decided to step back and make myself scarce. I slipped over to the wall that held all of Dr. Kinzel's diplomas. An undergraduate in psychology. Curious. That degree usually prepares one for a fruitful career manning the front desk of a dental office. Masters in English. OK, elevator repair... Ph.D... in music theory... well, at that point, why not?

I had paused at the music theory degree, though. Maybe that flare for the mellifluous was something that made Clark and Kinzel clash.

Oblivious to the grumbling tones that had gone on between Kinzel and Tuttle at this point, I turned to the two of them and said: "Hey, where's that coffee?"

You thought I was going to say something about the degree, didn't you?

The two of them turned their heads and looked at me like I

was spitting butterflies out of my mouth.

"Er, well... Yes. You're quite right. What sort of host am I? Let me just check on Sarah." Kinzel said, getting up from her chair at the table the two of them were sitting at.

"Tuttle! I just noticed something. Dr. Kinzel holds her Ph.D. in music theory." I said. Tuttle just looked at me with a blank look on his face. "Okay...?" Tuttle said with an expression that seemed as if he thought I was starting to smell like raw sewage.

"Don't you get it?" I asked "there may have been some conflict between the two of them. You know, because they were both into music?"

"Do you really think that the president of the university would kill a professor over a musical disagreement?" Tuttle asked sincerely.

"All I know is, I've seen some pretty passionate outbursts in my life over disagreements in music. If these two didn't like each other to begin with, who knows what could've sent one over the edge?" I said with a raised brow. "Why were you laying into Dr. Kinzel so hard, anyway, if you weren't suspicious of her?"

"Sometimes I just like to see how people react. You can learn a lot about someone that way." Tuttle said.

"I'm not sure you want to be getting too in the face of someone who might be a brutal killer!" I said, trying not to get too loud and animated. "Besides, I'm pretty sure she's not the killer." I told him.

"So, you still think Todd Monday is our man?" Tuttle asked.

"I'm not sure what I think." I said, though I did know one thing. We were still waiting for that coffee.

"Haven't the two of them been gone for quite a while?" I asked.

"Hmmm. You know what? You're right." Tuttle said, rising from a seated position, and poising to head out into the hall.

As Tuttle went out the door of the office, I followed behind. What we found was Dr. Kinzel at the desk of her secretary, hanging up the phone.

"Thank you, Detective Tuttle, but I won't be speaking with you anymore today. At least not without my attorney present." Dr. Kinzel said.

"If you don't have anything to hide, why do you need your attorney?" Tuttle said, and I could see the gears spinning in his head already.

"Good day, gentlemen." She said curtly.

"I don't suppose I can get that coffee to go?" I asked sheepishly.

This time, everyone looked at me a little off. At any rate, I think I should be able to get a coffee to go if they had promised me a coffee. Wouldn't you? Though, by the look on Tuttle's face...

"I'm sure there's a Starbucks on the way." I said.

*****

"That gal's got something to hide. I can feel it." Tuttle said as he scratched his neck and pulled at his collar, unbuttoned the top button and loosened his tie. The crisp fall leaves made several scraping noises as the wind blew them around the parking lot and across the sidewalk in front of us, crunching under our feet as we walked.

"Maybe, but she could've just been offended by your tone." I said with my most rib-poking voice.

"Are you kidding me? When I threw that in her face, she took the first chance she could get to run out of that room and call her attorney. She's got guilty written all over her!" Tuttle said, a grin beginning to spread across his face. I can see I wasn't going to change his mind on this. Actually, maybe I'm wrong and he's right. He is, after all, a professional. What do I know? I'm just a music store proprietor and a pretty sorry one at that! I haven't been back to my shop all day! It really would behoove me to get back there. That is, if I want to continue paying my bills and eating.

"Well, I'm going back to my shop for a while. Will you do me a favor?" I asked Tuttle.

"What?" he asked.

"Can you keep me in the loop on this? Let me know if you find out anything new?" I must've looked like a kid watching his dad go off to war.

"Sure, I guess." Tuttle said. "Whatever."

The two of us went our separate ways, and it surprised me to find how much I wanted to keep working on this case.

CHAPTER TWENTY-ONE

AFTER LEAVING KINZEL'S office, I was becoming more convinced that Todd, between his angry outbursts and his obvious motives, did indeed kill Dr. Clark. But the question was, how do we prove it?

Todd did say to me that he would "take care of it" when I talked to him on the phone. I suppose that could be taken as an admission of guilt. Then there was the incident at Dr. Clark's office. His violent outburst, throwing the chair at Dr. Clark, and just the wild mood swings in general, could lead one to believe that Todd Monday really could be Dr. Clark's killer.

It's obvious that Dr. Clark made Todd's life miserable, right from the get-go. He called her a monster, and worse. It was obvious that Dr. Clark had pushed Todd past his breaking point, but was that really enough to *kill*?

God knows people have killed for less.

I wish Michelle was here right now. She always had a way of calming me down and making me see things logically. I don't know how I would've got the music store off the ground if not for her. Every time things got crazy, or I got in a slump, or I just went kind of crazy and wanted to give up my dream, she always had a way of putting things in perspective. She was my center. My heart.

Focus, Jack. *Focus.* You're getting off course. Let's see now, Tuttle always says to bring him a plausible explanation. What would've happened after Todd ran out of Clark's office? So, Dr. Clark ran me out. Autumn Baylor told me she had seen Todd and Clark arguing just off stage during her concert. But about what? I can't imagine Todd would have been standing up to her backstage at a piano concerto. Besides, I got the distinct feeling that on that day in Clark's office, it was the first time Todd had ever let his true feelings out. Also, it would make sense that Todd would have the piano removed from campus. He knew exactly what that piano meant to Clark and the music program. If it didn't ruin Dr. Clark, and shut the program down, it would certainly torture her a little, which seems to be what Todd wanted to begin with.

But killing her? Maybe Todd didn't kill Dr. Clark out of anger and rage, but rather killed her because she found him out. Maybe Clark found out that it was Todd you had the piano stolen and put in the storage container. Maybe she found out where it was being held, showed up, and caught Todd red handed. When Clark showed up, and undoubtedly started spewing her usual venom and vitriol, Todd may have gone into another of his rages, pulled the prop out of the piano, and clubbed Dr. Clark in the head. He was certainly big enough to pick her up and put her in the piano by himself.

All the pieces were there! It really *did make sense!*

I was excited to take this to Tuttle and see what he had to say about my conclusion. Was he thinking the same thing, or was I way off base? It was time to find out.

CHAPTER TWENTY-TWO

I PUSHED THE doors open and walked hastily into the HGPD headquarters, stepped up to the front desk and ask for Detective Tuttle.

"Sir, can I ask what this pertains to?" The desk sergeant asked.

"I may have tied the pieces together in the Clark murder case." I said and sounded a little boastful, even to myself.

"Just a moment." The desk sergeant said, finding little excitement in my pronouncement. She was an attractive enough redhead with her hair pulled back and her uniform pressed crisp.

"I own the music store." I said, leaning in as if she had only known that in the first place she would have been more impressed. Her expression didn't change, however.

After a few moments passed, Tuttle came out and escorted me back to his desk. His desk was a mess, papers and folders everywhere, presumably case files. Tuttle's coat was laying across the back of his chair, and his gun was sitting in the top drawer of his desk, which sat open.

I took a seat in the small metal chair that was parked next to Tuttle's desk, facing him.

"Okay, what is it, Jack? What do you have?" Tuttle asked.

After I explained my theory to Tuttle, I stared at him, eyes wide and with bated breath.

"I'm impressed. You're pretty good! I gotta hand it to you, Jack, you put it together pretty well." Tuttle said. I was shocked. Tuttle was actually validating me!

"Here, look at this." Tuttle said, handing me a file. I flipped the manila file folder open, and on the top of the papers that were pinned inside was a statement from the storage company office. Long story short, the secretary of the storage unit company had given an affidavit to testify that Todd Monday was the name that was given when the unit that held the piano was reserved.

"We're moving forward with the case against Todd Monday. We're formally charging him with murder in the first degree against Dr. Brenda Clark." Tuttle said.

I couldn't believe it! Had I actually solved the murder on my own alongside a seasoned professional police detective? I was so excited that I hooted and slapped my knee. Tuttle laughed despite himself.

After heading back to my shop, I was sitting at my counter, reclining in my faux leather office chair, and noodling on a pristine Les Paul.

Sheila Bryant came down the stairs carrying the mail, sorting through it as she walked.

"Jack, I have your mail here. Mostly bills, of course." She said with a frown. "But there was also a letter. It looks like it might be a nice family letter or something. Do you write letters to your family? I love writing old-fashioned letters. Email is just so impersonal by comparison. I just…." She could see I was looking at her as she rambled and cut herself off. "Here you go." She handed me the handful of mail, sliding the letter in question off the top towards me.

I set the other letters aside and took out my pocket knife, flipped open the long blade, and used it to open the letter. As I unfolded the note inside, half expecting it to be some sort of insurance advertisement. I was surprised to see a handwritten letter. I mean, who hand writes stuff any more? I didn't recognize the writing. The note had been scrawled quickly, and almost illegible.

"What is it?" Sheila asked, no doubt rendered curious by my look of confusion.

"I'm not sure, really. It's kind of hard to read." I said. It was so bad, in fact, I began to mull over who I knew that was well versed enough in Sanskrit to translate it for me.

Well, maybe I'm exaggerating... a little.

After a few minutes of deciphering the letter in my hand, I began to make out that, at the very least, it wasn't a foreign language. I thought for a moment that a doctor had written me a letter. I began to realize, however, that the terrible handwriting was due to someone writing in a panic. They'd obviously given little attention to penmanship when they scribbled this note hastily on a regular enough looking piece of ruled notebook paper, and with what appeared to be just a plain old number 2 pencil.

The hastily scrawled chicken-scratch read, as far as I could tell:

Mr. Gulley,

I'm sorry you've gotten mixed up in this. I'm even sorrier I've gotten mixed up in this. I never meant for this to go as far as it has. Not sure why I'm writing this. The guilt is eating me up inside, maybe. If I don't tell someone, I'll go out of my mind. I just can't let Todd Monday go to jail for something he didn't do, but if it's found out I've told anybody anything they might kill me too.

Todd Monday is innocent.

There was no signature. Not even a monogram, like in the old mystery movies. The last line, however, stopped me in my tracks. *Innocent.* Todd Monday? Could this be fake? Sure, I suppose it could. But why? Why would someone come forward and confess? Well, they didn't actually confess. They seemed to know who committed the murder, though. Or did they? What if this was a letter sent by Todd himself, just a red herring to throw us off the trail? I was going crazy. What if I was wrong? What if Tuttle was wrong?

Rather than go into a panic by the thought that I was just a rank amateur, and that I was in way over my head and... as I was saying, rather than panic, I decided to share the letter with Tuttle to get a seasoned professional's viewpoint.

Here I was, once again, at the Harrow's Gate police department sitting next to a gentleman whom I was pretty sure had just wet himself. When the officer came and escorted the man to the back for questioning, it removed all doubt. I scooted down the bench in the opposite direction.

"Mr. Gulley?" It was the desk Sergeant again.

"Yes?" I responded.

"Do you need to see Detective Tuttle again?" The sergeant asked. I just sat there for a moment, struck by the attractive redhead I saw at the desk. She was looking at me attentively. A long, wavy wisp of red hair was hanging down in her face from an otherwise tightly pulled back mane that she quickly pulled back over her ear. The name plate on the desk read Sgt. Sarah Laney.

The last time I spoke with her, she was cute, no doubt. This time, she really caught my eye.

"Never mind, Sarah. I've got it." Tuttle said, coming around the corner of the station desk. "What is it now, Jack?"

"Is somebody playing Dreamweaver?" I asked under my breath.

"What?" Tuttle said, looking confused.

"I, uh, I got a letter." I said, trying to turn my attention to Tuttle, and speaking quietly, like I needed to keep a secret. "It's a bit hard to read, but it was the last line that got me."

Tuttle skipped to the end and raised a brow.

"Well, what do you think?" I asked him.

Tuttle just stood there, looking at the letter for a moment, then he motioned me towards the door to his office. Sarah smiled at me as I looked back at her while we moved into his office and I took a seat in front of his desk.

"Where did you get this? Have you shown it to anyone else?" Tuttle asked.

"Sheila, at the shop, is the only one who knows I have it, and she hasn't even read it. Who do you think it's from?" I asked.

"I have no idea, but I doubt it has any real relevance. Looks like a nut job wrote it. Maybe a junkie." Tuttle examined the paper, even sniffing it.

"There's no return address. Could be Todd Monday sent this himself, ever think of that?" Tuttle asked, looking at me with a raised brow.

To be perfectly honest, I *had* thought of that. I had to admit, that idea changed the way I thought about the letter. So what if it was Monday? What if he thought he could dupe us by simply sending us a letter that declared his innocence? Were we supposed to just read it and say, "Oh, well! It says here in this letter that Monday is innocent. Random letters from unknown authors are always proof of innocence in a court of law, aren't they?" He said with a bit of dramatic flair that, I must say, was evident of some amount of talent. I'll have to see if he could give some lessons to the theater group that put on that horrible play the other night.

"Well, yeah, I know it's not exactly irrefutable proof of his innocence…"

"It's not proof of anything, Jack, except that someone is trying to influence my investigation, whichever way they are trying to sway it." Tuttle said, changing his tone back to his normal, grumpy one.

"Look, I'll have forensics check it out and let you know if anything comes of it. I feel like it's a waste of time, but I'm a cop. I follow up on all my leads, even if I don't think it'll go anywhere."

All I knew was that *somebody* sent it. And that somebody knew more about what was happening with this investigation than the average Joe, or in this case, Mark. If they knew that Monday was going up the river for murder, it very well could be Monday sent the letter, or had someone send it, but something told me that this just wasn't the case. I couldn't put my finger on it, but I had to believe this was not Todd Monday's doing.

CHAPTER TWENTY-THREE

AFTER THE USUAL series of forensic fun conducted by the department came to no avail in the way of DNA, prints, or whatever they look for in those departments, Tuttle decided he would temporarily shelve the note until we had more to go on. He said he would need to know as soon as any other letters came to me no matter the time of day, and I agreed to the terms.

Now, at this point I was probably expected to go home, forget about the letter, forget about the murder for that matter, and just settle in to my chair and catch a ball game on TV while sipping my favorite beverage. And I planned to do that, I truly did, but it wasn't so easy for me to give up. To stop asking questions. I wanted to know. I *needed* to know.

My first stop was at the desk. The little redheaded desk sergeant was not at the desk, and while I was actually counting on this, I would be remiss to not mention here that I was a little bummed that she was not there.

So I found myself *"touring the facility,"* as it were. And if I were to happen to have a couple of grande caramel macchiato's, who would hold it against a guy sharing one of those with a lovely woman who has been known to enjoy a hot cup of Java? Certainly not me. I would admire such behavior. It's only good manners, isn't it?

"Hello?" I said as I knocked on the inside door to the M.E.'s office, holding the two macchiatos in a drink carrier at my side. Linda Raines was turned with her back to the door and started a little when I spoke.

"Who the heck are you? And who in the heck let you down here?" She asked with what can only be described as a combination of befuddlement and anger. Until she saw the macchiatos.

"Well, aren't you the bearer of good tidings? What can I do for you?" She asked, never taking her eyes off of the drinks.

"I'm Jack Gulley. I've been helping Detective Tuttle out on the Clark case. I was wondering if you'd be able to let me know anything you've learned?"

Tuttle had been winding down on filling out a grueling stack of paperwork when he finally decided to refill the coffee cup that had been sitting empty, drying out, but still smelling just strong enough to tickle his caffeine addiction into a ravenous fervor. Tuttle sat his pen down and rubbed his eyes. The urge to yawn was about to overtake him when he picked up the mug and headed downstairs to get that refill. Linda would have a lovely, hot, steaming brew of caffeinated bliss ready to fill the ceramic chalice he was gripping like a wide receiver catching the pigskin on game day.

Mmm... what is she brewing today? That smells amazing! Tuttle thought to himself as he quickly closed in on the door to the M.E.'s office.

Tuttle opened the door to what he recalled as a grim scene.

Jack was sitting on Linda Raines' desk, Linda seated in her chair, both sipping frothy coffee shop delicacies.

"Hey, Mark!" Jack said jubilantly, "Want some coffee?"

Tuttle gripped his mug even harder.

CHAPTER TWENTY-FOUR

"WHAT ARE YOU doing here, Jack?" Tuttle asked with all the concentrated restraint he could muster.

"Linda and I were discussing the Dr. Clark case. She found something I thought was very interesting. Wanna hear what it is?" I asked.

Tuttle wasn't looking so well. I was starting to think he might need to sit down. Or maybe he just needed to hit something?

"Mark, now don't get upset. Your friend here was just asking me a few questions. I figured he's been consulting, and helping you solve this case so..." Linda began, but Tuttle interrupted her. "*What?* Helping me *solve this case?* Don't make me laugh."

I have to say; I was a little offended. I was just about to say something when the good doctor spoke up and defended my honor.

"Now listen, Mark, this young man has brought you several angles you hadn't thought about looking at. You should have better manners, boy!"

"That's right, Mark." I said, but quickly regretted it when Tuttle's eyes narrowed and shot at mine. "Er, I mean Detective Tuttle."

Tuttle took a deep breath, shrugged his shoulders, and rubbed his face. "Okay, I'll concede that Jack has been a little help in this investigation. But to say he's helped *solve* the case is just wrong. It's still open." Tuttle said matter-of-factly. "He's a consultant. Nothing more."

Tuttle moved over to the nearest metal table and sat his still empty mug on it with a clank. Linda, rising from her chair and moving towards Tuttle, picked up the mug and put her hand on his face. "See, now was that so hard?" Linda then turned and headed for the coffeemaker on the table across from her desk and poured Tuttle's mug full of steaming hot coffee.

"Jack. Yes, I appreciate your contributions. But I'm a professional. You are not." Tuttle put his hands out to emphasize the point.

"And I am ever grateful for being given the opportunity to assist," I said, "and I think we might have a little something for you."

Tuttle glanced from me to Linda and back. Linda smiled and raised a brow. I slid off the desk, stepped over to where Tuttle was standing, and flipped the switch on the x-ray light box on the wall behind Tuttle.

The previously black sheet that was hanging on the box flickered into an image of a skull. I pointed at the left side of the skull.

"Well?" I asked, and waited for Tuttle to see it.

"What? What am I looking at?" He asked, pulling his jacket back and putting his fists on his hips, looking a bit like Peter Pan.

"Look at the damage to the skull, not the skull itself so much. What do you see?" I said while pointing out the area around the side of the skull where Clark had been hit.

Tuttle looked at the image, his eyes darting around the area I was pointing at. And then he stopped. "What? What am I supposed to see?"

"Look at the angle." I said.

Tuttle didn't seem enlightened by my suggestion. Linda stepped in and tried gently to give him a slight hint.

"The fracture on the side of Clark's skull is at an angle that says the person who clubbed her was not only left-handed, but…"

"Shorter! The killer was shorter than Clark!" I suddenly shouted. I could hardly contain myself. Linda and Tuttle both looked at me like I had ruined the punchline to a carefully told joke.

"Anyway, the angle of that particular blow is suggestive of

the suspect being shorter than Clark or maybe the blow was impromptu and they swung at her from close up and couldn't get an overhand arch to the swing and just hit at an upward arching angle. Either way, the angle is not how I would describe a blow from Todd Monday as looking. No. He would have more power in his swing, even if he held back. And the length of his arms wouldn't really allow for him to get the swing that he would need to do this kind of damage close up. It just doesn't add up." Linda explained while I nodded and admittedly fidgeted with excitement.

"So, you're saying that Monday probably didn't kill Clark." Tuttle said, finally piecing it together. "Good work, Linda."

"Not me!" Linda said and then nodded and looked in my direction.

"Just here to help, Tuttle." I said, raising my hands up and feigning modesty.

"Really?" Tuttle said, sounding simultaneously disbelieving and disappointed.

"Well, you don't have to sound so enthusiastic, buddy." My feelings weren't really hurt, but I was putting on a pretty good act. Tuttle just rolled his eyes.

"Thanks." He said with as little bravado as could be mustered. Honestly, I was happy he wasn't just outright abusive. The fact that he was indifferent towards my discovery was a relief.

"Manners!" Linda said, and lightly whacked Tuttle over the back of his head.

"Thank you, Jack. I couldn't have done it without you!" Tuttle said with heavy, albeit artificial, enthusiasm this time. I laughed a little. I couldn't resist. Linda laughed, too.

And then I thought I saw Tuttle grin, just a little, but a grin.

CHAPTER TWENTY-FIVE

I WAS OPENING some new guitars I had ordered for the shop window that sets up at street level. Sheila lets me use it, though it's deeded as a secondary window for the upstairs shop.

I got a call on my cell phone from Tuttle, so I answered, but wondered what he would want from me. After all, when he found me hanging out with Linda Raines in the Medical Examiner's Office, he almost blew a gasket.

"Hello?" I said with trepidation, half expecting to hear screaming from the other end as soon as I picked up.

"Jack. I wanted to let you know that what I said was true. I really do appreciate your... unique perspectives on this case."

"Oh! Well, uh... thanks! I guess?" I said. I wasn't sure what Tuttle had eaten, drank, smoked or injected, but I was curious about where this was going.

"Yeah, uh, listen, I was going to wait to tell you, since you seem to show up here at the station when no one has asked for you anyway, but Linda thinks I should let you know now. I had the guys go over the piano once more for prints. We found the same prints we expected from the original dusting, but this time we got a partial that we missed before."

"Really? Were you able to identify it?"

"No. There were no matches in the system. Also, the same prints were found on the piano lid stand that was used to kill Clark, just a partial again, but it matched the other. But that does tell us one thing for certain. Todd Monday is innocent. His prints were nowhere to be found on the Bösendorfer." Tuttle said. "And there's the fact that his credit card statement shows he purchased a hoagie across town about the same time as the murder occurred, so there's that…"

"Ah. Great detective work."

"Yeah, thought you'd like that."

We exchanged the usual niceties and got off the phone. Todd was innocent. It was great news to hear that the poor kid was exonerated, but that also left the giant question of who actually *did* kill Doctor Clark?

The thought had been bugging me; I couldn't shake the feeling that Todd, while being innocent of the murder of Brenda Clark himself, may know of some other individuals who may carry the burden of being in the wheelhouse of potential killers.

The day had receded into a dusk, the sunset just under the horizon now, still light but definitely not broad daylight.

I was curious as to exactly when, and how for that matter, they would explain to Todd Monday that he had been removed from the suspect list. Not being an officer myself, I have no idea what the procedure for something like that is. Do you just go up to the person in their cell and say "Hey, guess what. We messed up. Here's your stuff. Sorry to detain you for weeks. Hope you can put the pieces of your life back together! Here's a coupon for a free potato at the Sizzler!"

It's a curious thing, driving up to a guy's house that you helped put behind bars in order to ask him more questions about the same crime. I hope he doesn't go off on me. I know I probably deserve it if he does, but I'd much rather he just answer the door and say something like 'Hey, Jack! Long time, no see! How's it been?'

Nope. I won't put money on that scenario. I'll just hope for the best.

As my car came to a stop in the parking lot of Todd's apartment complex on the campus of Harrow's Gate University, I took a deep breath, held it, then exhaled slowly. I exited my car and walked to the door of Todd's apartment with a brisk step, trying not to chicken out of my so far holding resolve.

I knocked on Todd's door hesitantly, a grimace on my face as I did it. Maybe he won't be home, I thought for a moment.

Then he answered.

The door cracked open, the chain on the door still visibly in place. "What the heck do you want?" He asked me with a bit of biting tone in his voice.

"I started to say something witty or charming, then thought better of it. "I'm sorry, Todd. I really am. I'm glad you were cleared of all charges, though."

"Yeah. Not nearly as glad as I am." Todd said, cooly.

"So, I was really here to ask if you knew of anyone else who might have had any motive to kill Dr. Clark?" I asked.

"Yeah. The line would start around the block."

"Oh, I see. So who is on your short list, say the top three?" I asked.

Todd looked a little impatient and glanced around a bit before answering my question.

"Look, I don't know who killed Dr. Clark. I might say to take a look at the President of the school, I don't know." Todd said dismissively.

"Well, we're already looking into her, or rather the police are." I said, "What can you tell me that might explain why she would want her dead?"

"There was always some sort of weird tension between them, like Dr. Clark was hiding something and the President was covering for her. Or maybe it was the other way around. I don't know, but sometimes they would be talking in Dr. Clark's office, and when they saw me close by they would close the door."

"Didn't you say that you heard them arguing sometimes?" I asked.

"Yeah, usually it was after they closed the door, though. I assume it was about the music program going in the tank, though." Todd said, sounding a little more lively now.

"Was there ever a time that they may have said anything that might have given you a clue as to why they wanted to keep the music program's problems a secret? Even when it was something that everyone seemingly knew about, anyway?" I asked him.

Murder in the Key of M

"No idea why it was so secretive. I never heard anything else. The rest of the time, I guess she was taking whatever they were arguing about out on me. I gotta go. I hope you get your man. I'm just glad you realize it ain't me now." Todd said and then slammed the door in my face.

While I was walking back to my car, I saw what looked like someone standing around the corner of Todd's building. When I looked in that direction, the person who had been there was gone. Had someone been listening to our conversation?

I didn't have time to figure it out, and I needed to get back to the house. It was dark now and the day I was going to have tomorrow required an actual night's sleep. I was taking part in a music festival at the fair site. There was supposed to be some splendid music acts there and loads of vendors. I was there as one of the latter. My shop had been signed up since the festival was announced. It was my hope that I might be able to sign up several people for guitar lessons. Piano lessons might be in poor taste considering the recent turn of events in town.

Anyway, I needed to be well rested for the day. I was backing out of the parking spot I was in and I saw it again. A silhouette of a figure against the fading light of the night sky. As I flipped on my headlights, the figure quickly shot back behind the building. I threw my car into park and jumped out and ran to the corner of the building where I had just seen the figure standing. By the time I made it there and looked around the side of the building, there was no one to be seen. I slowly walked back to my car, getting semi-blinded by the headlights in my face in the process. I got back in my car, pulled the seat belt over my shoulder and clicked the buckle. While my eyes were still adjusting, I took my left hand off the wheel and slipped it over to the door to press the button that would lock the car, only realizing then how startled I had been when the sound of the locks clicking into place made me jump.

I drove home watching every dark corner and looking down every alley, half expecting to see the shadowy figure darting around the corner and out of sight again, or worse, coming right

109

at me.

The next morning, I woke up extra early to get ready for the music festival. Scratch that, it would be more accurate to say that I got up extra early, as I had not slept much at all. My mind had been racing all night between talking to Todd and the mysterious silhouetted figure that seemed to be stalking me last night. An extra large cup of coffee and I was off.

I had to say, just sitting in my car brought back some of the chills I had tonight before. But I had a job to do. I needed to get to this music festival and sign some kids up for guitar lessons. But something about what Todd said kept scratching at the back of my head. I couldn't quite place exactly what it was that he said, but something just seemed off. Not about Todd, but something he *said* had left me uncomfortable. But this would have to wait till later. Like I said, I had a job to do.

As I pulled into the parking lot of the festival, I was still thinking about what Todd said in spite of myself. It wouldn't hurt anything if I just thought about this a little bit, would it?

I set up my booth and put out my signs and waited for the people to start arriving. There were several other booths, one of which was for the music program at the University. It surprised me they would have representation considering that they had just lost their program director, and not in a 'took another job' kind of way, but in the dead kind of way.

I was curious who would be tending to the booth, so I headed over to say hello. As I got closer to the booth, I could see a familiar face. It appeared that Autumn Baylor had been tapped to represent Harrow's Gate University's Music program, though, with a dead program director and a reputation for bad luck with near priceless instruments, one would imagine it could be a hard sell. I decided to go say hello and wish them luck, anyway.

"Autumn, how are you? So, did Dr. Kinzel send you down here, or are you here on your own?" I asked sincerely.

"I'm here on my own." Autumn said with a hint of guilt." I felt it would be a good way to honor Dr. Clark, you know?"

"Well, that is certainly very admirable of you. I know you must want to do whatever you can to help preserve the program that got you where you are today." I said.

"Yes, but more so, this is for Dr. Clark herself. I really wanted to do this for her." Autumn said mournfully, looking down at the table.

"Well, I think it's wonderful that you're here. I'll tell you what, if someone comes to my table and wants to learn more than just a few guitar lessons, I'll be sure to send them your way." I said with a smile. Autumn smiled back, but only for a second, like the polite smile someone gives you at a funeral. I just smiled back and headed back to my table.

On the way back, I saw another of the tables set up by the University and grabbed a brochure. Maybe it was time for me to go back to class.

CHAPTER TWENTY-SIX

THE FAIR WAS going well. I had signed up several folks for music lessons and had one gentleman ask me about ordering him a custom Gibson Les Paul. I was enjoying getting back to my roots.

I had felt like I had been neglecting the business for the last few weeks, what with the Bösendorfer theft, Dr. Clark's murder, and Todd Monday being released, I had been out of my shop quite a bit. It felt good to get back to my element. It also was giving me time to think about getting some help in the shop, so I pulled my phone out since traffic had slowed at my booth for a few minutes and placed an ad on the local newspaper's website. Now all I have to do is wait for the applications to roll in.

As I finished placing my ad and wiped the fresh fingerprints from the screen of my smartphone with the hem of my shirt, I noticed Autumn Bayless was packing up her stuff and loading it into her car. I was watching her from my booth and wondered when Andrea Keller was going to show up, and without even having to say her name, the little devil appeared.

I couldn't hear what they were saying, of course, but I could definitely see them exchanging some conversation while Autumn packed and Andrea watched her. I must have come up, because Andrea turned and looked at me quite purposefully. I don't know what she was thinking, but she made no expression one way or the other. I was curious, though, as to why those two were always together. I had to get away from my roomie in college. He would drive me nuts if I didn't! I really liked him, don't get me wrong, but he had to be taken in small doses. He collected Beanie Babies. And not in a healthy way. Apparently, these two girls did not have that problem. They seemed to go everywhere together.

I raised my hand and gave a courteous wave and nod to Andrea. She just laughed, furrowed her brow and turned her head away with a smirk that spoke volumes about her feelings toward me, like she couldn't believe I would have the gall to wave at her. As Steve Martin used to say: "Well, excuuuuuse me!"

I want to believe she has a LOT of Beanie Babies.

I decided that the fair was winding down, and it was getting late, so I started packing up my things as well. The papers and brochures I had laid out on my little table, covered with a black faux leather tablecloth, were quickly stashed away, and the tablecloth folded up easily. I had the table packed up in no time and the marketing materials and table covering tucked into a plastic tote.

On the way to put stuff from my table back in my car, I picked up a pamphlet from another vendor. It was a community college. A particular program caught my eye. Private Investigator. The thought of being a legitimate investigator and being able to help the police with cases appealed to me. It was a side of me I'd never known. Music is my passion in life, but I had been having so much fun helping Tuttle in this case, I couldn't imagine getting bored. I put the brochure in my back pocket, folding it into a neat square first. I'd look that over later.

The trunk of my car was filled with things that I had been leaving back there for years. It was like the trunk of a hoarder. Unfortunately, there were no duffle bags containing a million bucks back there. Oh, well. Maybe someone else would need a trunk to leave a duffle bag containing a million bucks in. Maybe they'd split it if they could use my trunk. It was at that moment that I realized that I had really been fantasizing about a random person leaving a million bucks in my car for far too long.

I was right; it was time to go home. I was obviously more tired than I thought.

CHAPTER TWENTY-SEVEN

TODD MONDAY HAD only been out of jail for two days now. On the first day that he was out, he was visited by Jack Gully, who, for one reason or another, still had questions regarding Dr. Clark's murder. Todd couldn't believe that there were any more questions to be asked by the police, or anyone else for that matter. As Todd saw it, Clark had it coming. Why was it such a big deal?

Todd was raised in a Christian home and had Christian values, to be sure. But he also knew that Dr. Clark was not a good person, and at first he prayed for her and tried to overlook her constant berating of everything he did.

After a while, though, he found it all overwhelming. Todd couldn't find the strength to resist the contempt that was welling up inside him for Dr. Clark.

Todd continued to arrange his textbooks on the floor along the edges of the walls in a neat, methodical manner. He had this idea since his undergraduate program about arranging his books in such a way as to have a continuous flow of knowledge at his feet as he walked from room to room. He knew it was a little silly and probably just an excuse he told himself to avoid paying extra money for bookshelves, but hey, whatever works, right? Today was going to be about the books. Forget about the dead boss, the police, the accusations... all of it. Todd wanted to think today was about Todd. But the truth was, in reality, it wasn't.

Jack Gulley showing up to ask more questions worried Todd immensely. If this Jack Gulley guy was going to show up probing into Todd's life, even after he had been exonerated, how much further behind would the police be? Todd's anxiety grew, and he quickly lost interest in his books. He began to think that maybe he should lie low for a while, perhaps at a family member's home somewhere far away. Just for a while, until things blew over.

Todd began packing a bag he pulled from his closet, an old duffel bag he'd owned since he took a trip to Canada after his first year in college. It had a couple of frayed places on the strap, but other than that, the bag was in excellent condition. He unzipped all the pockets and began the process of emptying his drawers and stuffing the contents into the bag.

Once the bag was full, Todd began to think about what else in the apartment needed to be packed up. Other than a few essentials, he could think of nothing that would be of any major importance. Other than the picture of her. The one. The girl of his dreams. The one thing he would regret leaving behind. He has been in love with her since he was an undergraduate, and now the best thing he could do for her is leave. He knew he would come back for her. It was just a matter of when.

None of that mattered now, though. Todd needed to get away. He needed to distance himself from the investigation, the questions, and her. She would never understand if he said something to the police that would be incriminating. Of course, she wouldn't understand. She probably didn't even know he existed, but she would. She would know he exists, and she would realize that all he had done had been for her. Todd would see to it.

Todd thought he heard pounding on his door. He moved across the apartment to look through the peep hole. He saw a familiar face. For just a moment, Todd thought about opening the door. He decided against it. Maybe they would just leave.

There was no time to think about that right now. Soon, he would have to try to get back to some semblance of a normal life. The first thing to do would be to find a new job. Todd was sure he didn't have his old job anymore. Kind of a given when your boss has been murdered. If not for throwing a temper tantrum in her office and then being arrested for her eventual murder, innocent or not. Not that Todd wanted to work that job anymore, anyway. God only knew he was over that stage of his life. No, sir. Todd

Monday was setting out on his life's adventure. Clean slate.

Todd began to look at the books he had just finished lining up and ran his fingers through his hair, taking in a deep breath and exhaling slowly. He was just satisfied with how the books had been arranged.

Now to start over.

CHAPTER TWENTY-EIGHT

LIKE MANY PEOPLE, Andrea Keller had grown up in a small town where she went to high school, just like most kids do. She went to football games, school dances, and played flute in the marching band as well. She even went to church on Sundays with her family and assumed the usual teenage, ho-hum look on her face while the congregation sang hymns. She was an average, ordinary, everyday teenager.

But the days of pizza parties with friends, sleepovers while binging on ice cream and watching reality television until far too late into the night, were long gone.

Andrea remembered the events of three years ago that made such a change in her life clearly, and she could almost still taste the grease on the tater tots they served in the cafeteria. She could still smell the aroma of the distinctively shaped, rectangular pizza slice that sat on her tray just under her face, and she could still see the odd shape that the spout of her chocolate milk carton had taken after struggling to open it for over two minutes. Her boyfriend, Nathan, had offered to help, but Andrea wanted to do it herself. She couldn't explain it because in truth she didn't understand it herself, but she felt patronized when Nathan offered to help her with anything. She knew that he was just trying to help and that it was just something boyfriends did for their girlfriends. And she knew Nathan was a great guy, but she couldn't help but be put off by him sometimes.

The school had an assembly that ran long that morning, so the lunch periods had to be blended between the sophomores and juniors. That was the day Andrea met Lisa. She'd noticed her come into the cafeteria, her long blonde hair draped over one shoulder, her hands gripping the corners of her tray as she stepped in line for her slice of pizza and greasy tater tots. She wasn't sure what it was about this girl, but she smiled. She had a feeling that they could be friends. Maybe she reminded her of a kid she knew when she was younger. Maybe she seemed like herself not too long ago, when she was new to the school. Whatever it was, this new kid made her smile. Andrea hadn't been smiling much lately, and she surprised herself. She surprised Nathan, too.

"What's got into you?" He asked.

"I don't know. I guess it's just this day is so crazy with all these people crowded into the cafeteria. It's just kind of nuts." Andrea replied, brushing off Nathan's inquiry.

As the blond girl paid for her lunch and turned with a thousand-yard stare across the sea of faces and tables, it became obvious she was at a loss for where to sit. As she slowly stepped between the crowded roundtables, her eyes scanned the room and the corner of her mouth curled. Of course, Andrea noticed this, she'd been watching her the entire time. Then it occurred to her to wave the girl down and offer her a seat. As Andrea stood and raised her hand, Nathan cast a confused look at her as if she had just jumped up and started singing a rounding chorus of Yankee Doodle Dandy.

"What are you doing?"

"Offering that girl a seat."

"Why?"

"Because she needs one."

"Why?"

Andrea gave Nathan a look that said it all. With one glance, she told him he was being rude and that she'd have no part of it. Nathan had been with Andrea long enough to know that you choose your fights with her, and this wouldn't be one of them.

As the blond girl apprehensively approached the table, Andrea smiled at her with as much warmth and kindness and she could muster. Nathan grinned and nodded, but never quite made eye contact.

"Don't mind him. He's just shy." Andrea said dismissively, motioning to an empty seat with her hand and clearly indicating for the girl to sit down.

"I'm Lisa. Thanks for the seat."

"No problem!" Andrea said, and even she felt she had said it a little too enthusiastically. "My name is Andrea, and this is Nathan." Nathan just nodded. "You a sophomore? Is that why I've never seen you at lunch before?"

"Yeah, I guess." Lisa said.

The rest of lunch went along well, as one would expect. The usual line of conversation among teenagers. However, one thing was very different about after lunch. Andrea Keller realized that she really liked this Lisa girl. She needed a friend to hang out with that wasn't her boyfriend. Someone to talk to about stuff you just don't want to talk to boyfriends about. Someone to share your darkest secrets.

After that day at lunch, in the days and weeks that followed, Andrea made sure to go out of her way to say hello to Lisa in the halls. She made sure to invite her to activities after school and on weekends. She even arranged slumber parties so she could invite Lisa over to her house. And the two made fast friends.

The girls had made a day of shopping at the mall, eating greasy hamburgers at the popular burger spot among the high school set, and then ran back to Andrea's place to watch movies all night in her room. They talked about school, music, movies, and books they had read. Even boys they liked. "But don't tell Nathan I said that." was a common tagline from Andrea. They planned exactly what they wanted their weddings to be. Andrea said she wanted to get married in a grassy pasture in a beautiful dress, and Lisa said she wanted to get married in a large church ceremony with hundreds in attendance. The movies always ended up as background noise as sleep overtook Lisa quickly after the activities of the day had exhausted her.

As Lisa slept, Andrea watched her. She wasn't sleepy, so she thought about her friend and, indeed, their friendship. She was certain that Lisa was her best friend, but now she was ready to test their bond. She wanted to see what Lisa thought about her friend when she was in private; behind the veil, as it were.

Andrea slowly crept over to Lisa's things, opened her Dooney & Burke purse, pulled out her phone, and tapped the screen. Lisa didn't have a passcode on the phone, but Andrea knew it would be Cotton3677, the name of her poodle and the birth date of her mother. She used it on all her devices. But that was something only the best of friends would know.

Andrea started scrolling through Lisa's texts, looking for a mutual friend or someone similar that they had in common, hoping to see if Lisa thought as much of her friendship as she did.

Lisa had texts to people Andrea didn't know, and family members, but she hadn't come across any messages referring to her yet.

Then she saw a familiar name.

Nathan.

Strange... she thought. *Why was she texting Nathan? Nathan wasn't very friendly to Lisa when they were all together. Strange they would text anything to each other.*

Andrea read the feed, scrolling down and down. It was a substantial thread. Her heart broke more with every swipe of her finger. It wasn't even the infidelity of Nathan that hurt so much. She knew she and Nathan were never going to last forever. That was doomed eventually anyway, but the worst part was the betrayal she felt from Lisa. She was her friend. Her *best* friend.

How could she stab her in the back like this?

Andrea saw red. She kicked her foot into Lisa's side, inducing a winded "Oof!" from Lisa.

"What is this?!?" Andrea yelled, shoving the phone into Lisa's face.

"Why are you looking at my phone? That's my private stuff! How dare you?!?" Lisa shouted back, sounding hurt and angry as well.

"You're trying to steal my boyfriend!! How dare *you*?!?" Andrea screamed back, in tears by now.

Lisa grabbed her phone, picked up her things and scrambled out, heading home, in tears herself at that point.

For Lisa, the next week was one of feeling something between shame and heartbreak, confusion and yearning for things to just be like they were before. Andrea was full of feelings that conflicted, yet worked in tandem to make her head swim. The rest of the time was spent passing awkward stares in Lisa's general direction, and Lisa avoiding eye contact at every cost.

Lisa had stopped talking to Andrea altogether. The fact that Andrea kept showing up everywhere she went, quite frankly, made her very uncomfortable. She felt uneasy about how Andrea seemed to know just where, and when, Lisa would be on any given day, and always seemed to be there, staring at her.

As the end of the year came closer, Lisa had tried her best to move on and forget the whole ugly ordeal. She had even started talking to a boy on the football team. Evan was a receiver, and she would scream from the bleachers for him when he would take the ball into the end zone at Friday night football games, making the game-winning touchdown, or sometimes just keeping the team from leaving a game without ever making it on the board, either way, Lisa screamed just as loud. She wasn't screaming for the team or even the school. She was screaming for Evan. Lisa knew he was talking to some mutual friends about asking her to the prom, too. She knew she would say yes, but she was excited to play coy, anyway.

It was Thursday. The sun was shining, and the bleachers were casting hard shadows on the pavement. The wind was a little brisk, but Lisa enjoyed the breeze. She could hear the shuffle of her feet on the ground as she fiddled with the zipper of her backpack, trying desperately to get the bag to close after squeezing in the last book she needed from the library for a paper she was writing for her Honors English class. She could hear the cries of the soccer players on the field as they ran drill after drill, and the calls of the coach as he tried to get someone who was apparently making an egregious error with their footwork to "cover those feet".

Her shuffling sounded different as she gained distance from the field and the bleachers. She could almost make a dragging sound out. She stopped walking and the shuffle of her own feet went silent, but shuffling persisted, if only for a moment. Lisa knew immediately that there was someone behind her. She could feel the hair on her neck stand on end, and goosebumps covered her arms. That she could feel, and almost hear, the now racing beat of her own heart rising in her throat as the very thought spilled from her mind, made her all the more terrified. It was fight or flee, only she couldn't do either. She just froze. She wanted to scream, but the only sound she could make was a pathetic squeak that sounded more akin to a pet toy than a cry for help.

Then it started. It was as if one of the professional wrestlers her brother watched on TV tackled her. Lisa felt disoriented, not knowing what was really happening but feeling every punch, claw, kick and bite. The noise was almost worse. It was deafening, a wail like a banshee, screaming its mournful cry. The fury of the beating was disorienting, the pain unbearable. Lisa was feeling the sensation of things that had already happened. She knew they had already happened, but in the flurry of painful blows, she somehow wasn't registering the pain in real-time. It was even more terrifying when she first realized that her lung had been pierced when she was having trouble breathing, though she wasn't sure of which broken rib had made it that far in. Her nose was broken, and her eye was cut, not the brow, but her eye itself was actually cut. She couldn't hear anymore. The blows and clawing were all making a dull thumping noise now, and she could feel the swelling increase, seemingly everywhere. She was starting to have trouble concentrating now. And sleepy... so very... sleep...

Lisa felt her head pounding. She felt the sheets of the bed she was in and immediately felt uncomfortable. This wasn't her bed. But it was more than that. The mattress felt lumpy and unwelcoming. The pounding was increasing. She tried to open her eyes, but they seemed heavy, and one was swollen shut. When her good eye gained focus, she saw an unfamiliar room. The television hanging on the wall had some news show playing that Lisa didn't recognize. Her arms were heavy, and she felt the tight spot in the bend of her arm that she could now see was where an IV was placed. She followed the tube running from her arm to the machine on a metal pole that had an IV pump attached to it that was standing next to her bed.

She also saw Andrea next to her bed in a chair, asleep.

Had she stayed the whole time? In spite of their clear issues, and the confusion of what the actual nature of their relationship was after everything that had transpired, Andrea had always been a reliable friend.

Lisa cleared her throat.

Andrea woke with a start.

"Lis'?" Andrea said, sounding surprised and groggy.

"Hey." Lisa tried to say, but her throat was so dry, she merely mouthed the word with a raspy passing of air.

Andrea hit the call light and stood up next to the bed.

"Hey! I'm so sorry this happened to you. Are you hurting? What do you remember? Do you know what happened?..." she was throwing all this at Lisa in a manner that Lisa had to interject.

"Slow down." She managed to rasp, her throat beginning to moisten again.

"I'm sorry." Lisa said. "I shouldn't have pushed you away so hard. You were justified to be mad. You were still my friend. I was just..."

"No, no, no... you don't have anything to be sorry about. I should never have pushed... I'm the one who's sorry." Andrea said in a rushed voice.

The nurse came into the room. "Alright! Our patient is awake! Excellent! Do you need anything for pain? What's your pain level on a scale of one to ten, ten being the worst pain you've ever felt?"

"Maybe a six." Lisa replied

The girls' conversation put on hold, Andrea sat back in the chair, looking relieved.

"What happened to me?" Lisa asked the nurse.

The nurse picked up Lisa's hand and began looking at the clock on the wall, staying silent for several seconds, obviously taking Lisa's pulse, but inadvertently leaving the question hanging in the air, finally turning back to Lisa, saying "Honey, you were a victim of an assault it seems. The police are going to want to talk to you."

Lisa looked at Andrea, silently seeking confirmation. Andrea just looked sad. Lisa wanted to tell Andrea not to be sad, she was going to be okay. Instead, the pain medicine that the nurse had injected into the IV line was quickly taking effect, and Lisa found, her head not pounding so hard anymore, that she was quickly nodding off again.

CHAPTER TWENTY-NINE

AUTUMN BAYLOR SLID the shackle through the hole in the locker latch. She had just been to Honors English and was headed to her favorite class, Advanced Piano Sight Reading. She was deemed gifted at an early age on the piano, so the class was her way to make piano interesting and challenging. The class was part of an individualized curriculum that the school had created for Autumn. It was her senior year of high school and she was hoping to get a music scholarship to Harrow's Gate University the following year. Dr. Clark was notorious for running potential scholarship representatives through their paces.

The sight reading was not your usual hymns from church or even traditional piano pieces. The music was chosen specifically to be difficult to just pick up and play, though her instructor had found Autumn to be especially adept at tackling difficult pieces.

Her guilty pleasure was certain jazz pieces. The difficulty was in the changing keys and time signatures, not to mention the almost random selection of notes to the untrained ear. It was pure bliss to Autumn.

And while Autumn could be painfully shy at times, she was trying hard to be more social. The only time she felt the social anxiety slip away was when she was at the piano. Even on stage, she could lose herself in the music and the entire world would fade out. At that point, it was just her and the piano, her hands, and the music.

Today had been particularly trying for her. The kids had all been talking to her about the recital that was scheduled for Thursday evening. Everyone wished her good luck, and some even said they would be there.

Oh, God. She thought. All she could think about was the people staring at her in expectation. She wasn't worried about being good. That was easy. She was, instead, terrified by the thought of people. People staring, talking with and trying to converse with and congratulate her. It almost gave her hives.

Autumn took a deep breath, held it for a moment, and let it out.

Her therapist had talked to her about this. It would be good for her. She needs to learn to socialize. To come out of her shell, even just a little bit. At least the music would be there. It is her safe zone; her zen.

Autumn had tried organized sports as a kid. Being from Philadelphia, her parents thought cricket would be a fine, organized sport for her to get involved in. There was also an air of refinement to cricket over something else, like softball, which in their eyes was low-brow.

To say that Autumn came from money would be an understatement. Her family was fabulously wealthy. To the point that even Autumn didn't fully understand the extents. All she knew was that her father had set up a trust that would allow her to "Do what your heart desires" as her father put it.

The cricket never worked out. Autumn was talented as a batter, but her social anxiety left her unable to handle the interaction of the coach and team.

Autumn didn't mind, though. It just gave her more time with her first love. The piano was her oasis. Her ability to play for hours tirelessly was both amazing and infuriating to her parents. Sometimes they would have to get out of bed at night to tell her to stop playing and go to sleep.

The reason Autumn played for so long was not that she needed the practice. No. Autumn needed the solace. She could simply not deal with the reality that surrounded her. That reality was that she was an honors student and musical prodigy that was expected to readily become valedictorian of her class, and while the studies and the music came easily to her, the social expectations that went along with it did not. The mere thought of having to make a speech to her entire graduating class and their combined family and friends, as well as the staff, faculty, and administration of the school, was enough to make her nauseous and she was sure she would break out in hives on the day of that event.

So she played. She played to get away from it all. She wondered if she could just play instead of giving a speech. No. She would be expected to do what they typically do. Autumn hated typical. And as much as she was told she was not at all typical, she felt typical. She felt boring, bland and, even though she had been given more than enough of her own attention from boys who would try to talk to her, unattractive. She knew that some of her feelings would not be considered accurate by others, but that was how she felt. Whether that was accurate really made no difference to her.

Autumn felt the pressure, too. Even though the grades were not that hard to keep up, she wished that they did not hold her up to that standard, whatever that standard was. And she also wished she could just talk to someone about everything.

Autumn was so tightly wound she felt she could burst like one of those watermelons they wrap rubber bands around until they explode.

Autumn was still sitting at the piano, though she hadn't been playing it since her mother had asked her to go to bed. Again. It was the third time this week.

She quietly and slowly lowered the fall board over the keys and gently pushed the bench back and headed for the stairs.

Autumn quietly stepped up the stairs and headed to her room. She enjoyed listening to the familiar creaks of the steps as she lightly stepped up the stairs and down the hall to her room.

As she slipped into her nightgown, brushed her teeth, and brushed her hair, she tried to unwind from the day and not think about the fact that it would all start again tomorrow.

She laid her head down on the pillow and sighed.

Autumn reached over to the small lamp that lit her

nightstand and switched it off by pulling at the small chain that hung from under the shade.

Finally, in the still silence of the dark, she could let it all go and finish her nightly routine.

Imagining the audience, a standing ovation, the stage lights, it was her concert, and she was duly appreciated by the crowd.

Eventually, she would sleep. Restful, silent sleep.

CHAPTER THIRTY

BY THE TIME I reached the shop, I had shifted my thoughts to the Bösendorfer. I started thinking about why someone would try to steal it, to begin with. Sure, it was ridiculously valuable, but there lies the rub. Who would you sell it to? A stolen piano of that value would be like trying to fence the Golden Gate Bridge. Well, maybe that was an exaggeration, but essentially true, at least in our little burg. We'd been looking at the murder of Clark so much we had stopped really thinking about the piano. If my thinking was correct, then if we found out who stole the piano, we find our killer. So I started trying to piece it all together.

While I was thinking about the case, I pulled out the brochure I had picked up at the booth the other day. I keyed the address of the website to the Private Investigator Licensure program into my computer behind the counter and started looking at tuition and the requirements of the program. I was feeling a little overwhelmed by the required time and work I'd have to put in to be a legit P.I. when Tuttle came in the door of the shop with two uniformed officers behind him.

"To what do I owe this unexpected visit?" I said to him jovially, shaking off the cold sweat I was forming while imagining myself trying to go back to school at my stage of life.

"You can dispense with the pleasantries Jack, this isn't a social call," Tuttle said with a very direct tone. I didn't like it. What he said, nor the tone.

"What's going on?" I asked, the concern in my voice apparently growing.

"We'll talk about it at the station, Jack. Do you have a lawyer? I can have Bryant call him for you." Tuttle said as he pulled my hands behind me and slipped cuffs on my wrists.

As if on cue, Sheila Bryant slowly and uneasily started down the stairs to my shop. "What's happening, Jack? What's going on? Why are the police here?" she said.

"You have the right to remain silent…" one of the uniformed officers said. I tried to speak, but nothing came out. I think my jaw moved, but when the words failed to come out, it just hung there, slack jawed. To say I was stunned would be an understatement. What was happening? Why was I being arrested?

"Anything you say can and will be held against you in a court of law…" he continued.

I tried to think, to imagine what I was being arrested for. Taxes? No, paid. Parking tickets? Jaywalking? Pretending to be an officer? That was it! I bet that's it! Oh, God! I'm being arrested for pretending to be a police officer!

"You have the right to an attorney. If you cannot afford an attorney, one will be appointed for you."

No, that can't be it. But what? What the heck was going on??

"Do you understand your rights as I have read them to you?" The officer finished.

I just looked at Tuttle.

"Do you understand your rights as I have read them to you?" He said again. I just nodded affirmatively, still shocked by what was happening.

Tuttle looked at me and just shook his head. He looked disappointed, whether in me or himself, I couldn't tell. If it was on me, I had no idea why.

"You're under arrest for the murder of Todd Monday." Tuttle said.

My jaw dropped, and for once, I couldn't speak. Remaining silent was somehow not a problem at this point.

All I could do was play this out and see what happened. That probably meant going to the station and being booked.

As the officer put me into the squad car, I couldn't really think about much of anything except what I was doing right before this all happened.

I wonder if being arrested at the same time you are looking into taking classes for becoming a private investigator would look bad on your college application?

CHAPTER THIRTY-ONE

DESK SERGEANT SARAH Laney was wide-eyed as they brought me through the front doors of the police precinct.

"Jack?" she said. "What happened? Did you get in trouble somehow? Mark, why did you arrest Jack?" the desk sergeant asked while coming around the desk, sounding both alarmed and confused.

Tuttle just looked forward and did not reply to Sarah. I simply shrugged and mouthed out *I have no idea* to her.

We moved down the hallway and back to the interrogation room we had previously questioned Todd Monday in.

The cold stainless steel table and chairs in the interrogation room were very different looking when it was me sitting at the table, soon to be across from the detective who was, heretofore, someone I thought of as a friend.

What I didn't know was why I was there. Surely Tuttle didn't believe I could kill Todd Monday, or anyone for that matter.

"Jack, I'm not going to mince words here." Tuttle said as he swiftly moved into the room and took the chair directly across from me. "We were given credible reports that you were seen visiting Todd Monday at his apartment. Is that true?" Tuttle said pointedly.

"Well, yeah. I guess so. Why? Is that a problem?" I asked, hoping I had broken some archaic law or rule about contact with previous suspects in a murder investigation, and that I had just misunderstood the Tuttle when he said I was under arrest for murder.

"Well, Jack, that depends on whether or not Todd was still alive when you left his apartment." Tuttle said while looking at me and passing a plain manilla folder to me. I flipped it open and saw a couple of photos of Todd Monday. He was obviously dead, and obviously not by natural causes. He'd been murdered, for sure.

"What happened?" I asked in disbelief.

"You tell me." Tuttle said, sitting down across from me.

"You think *I* did this? Are you crazy?? I couldn't kill someone. I can't even clean the giblets out of the turkey at Thanksgiving!" I said, almost shouting now. "Why would you think I killed him??"

Tuttle just looked at me and then rolled his eyes. "This morning an officer went to do a welfare check at Todd's dorm room after reports of shouting came in from another student upstairs who was trying to study. When the officer got to the scene, Monday's door was open, and he was laying across a pile of books, dead. He'd been bludgeoned. The question, Jack. Answer it. What happened when you were at Monday's apartment?"

"Well, I certainly didn't kill him, if that's what you think!" I said.

"Then just tell me the truth, Jack. Why were you there?" Tuttle pressed.

"I was just there to see if he'd tell me his short list of possible suspects. You know, since he was cleared I thought maybe he'd talk to me since I'm not a cop." I plead my case to Tuttle and hoped he'd let up a little. He didn't.

"Why did you feel like he'd tell you anything he hadn't already said? Don't you think he'd want to be completely open to the police when his neck was on the line? What made you think he'd tell you something new? That doesn't make a lot of sense, Jack. Why were you there? For real?" Tuttle pushed the table a little. I'm sure it was a tactic to make me sweat. It was working.

"What about that letter? Why would I bring you that letter saying Monday was innocent if I was planning on killing him? Seems like that would be kinda stupid, doesn't it? Dammit, Mark. I just asked him a couple of questions and then I left. Honest!

I never even went in the apartment." I said, sounding weary to even myself. My head dropped, and I slumped back in my chair. I probably looked defeated. I felt defeated, so I have no doubt that it manifested in my appearance as well.

I was taken back to my cell and spent the next few hours just sleeping. I have found that when I get extremely stressed, I just get very sleepy. Maybe my brain thinks that if I just go to sleep, all the bad stuff will be gone when I wake up.

The cell itself was pretty spartan. It had a bed that suspended from the wall, and a small stainless steel sink and toilet, as well as a tiny desk with a small stool that extended from underneath. I could see myself writing letters to people on the outside at that desk. I started wondering if I should get a tear drop tattoo off the corner of my eye. Then I started wondering what gang I would align myself with for protection. And I didn't want to even imagine shower days.

It was at this point I realized I had done nothing wrong and I wouldn't be going to prison for murder.

That never happens in real life. Right?

At least I hoped I wouldn't go to prison. The honest truth was, I had no idea what was going to happen to me. And then I was back to being terrified.

So I went back to sleep.

CHAPTER THIRTY-TWO

SARAH LANEY FINISHED her shift and followed the stairs up to the landing just outside the holding cells for the GCPD.

She opened the key box on the wall just outside the steel door to the cell row walkway, pulled the appropriate key out and unlocked the door to the lockup, and entered. A flood of memories came back to her as she entered the long corridor. When she started working for HGPD she was a corrections officer and spent her first two years on the force in this jail. Harrow's Gate wasn't really the kind of place to get hardened criminals, but rather the occasional guy who'd downed too many drinks and started thinking he was Steven Segal, then started acting like him too. He would eventually piss someone off bad enough that punches were thrown, one thing leads to another, and they'd get hauled in. She seemed to remember maybe even a petty thief or two.

Sarah slowly walked past the usuals, drunk and disorderliness, domestic squabblers who needed a night to cool off... then she came to Jack's cell.

"Hey." Sarah said softly, as she leaned on the bars to Jack's cell.

"Oh. Hey." Jack replied. "Sarah. I didn't do this."

Jack seemed heartbroken. Sarah's heart broke, too, when she heard the weariness in his voice and the look in his eye.

"I believe you, Jack." She said, trying her best to sound comforting, but knowing there's little comfort when you're sitting in a cell, waiting to be questioned for a murder.

"Thank's, Sarah. But right now I really need Tuttle to believe me." Jack said.

"I'm sure Tuttle wants to believe you, but he's in charge of a murder investigation that seems to have more questions than answers right now. He has to follow all roads, even when those roads lead to suspects he'd rather they didn't. Even when they lead to friends." Sarah said.

"If he thinks of me as a friend, why doesn't he talk to me about this as a friend, not like I'm a perp?" Jack said, sounding stressed.

"He can't afford to be seen as showing favoritism. You've got to understand." Sarah said.

Jack stood up to face Sarah, resting his hands in front of him on the crossbars. "I've only ever tried to help in this investigation, Sarah. That's all."

Sarah put her hands on Jacks. Both of them stood there for a moment.

"Jack," Sarah said softly, "let Mark follow procedure. He'll clear you. Just trust the process."

Jack looked Sarah in the eyes. He saw her sincerity and took a deep, cleansing breath.

"Okay." Jack said finally.

"Okay." Sarah replied with a tight-lipped smile.

Jack melted a little. He hadn't meant to show it, but he was sure he had. And he was correct in his assumption.

Sarah blushed.

"Gotta go." She said, moving back a step, but leaving her hands on Jacks.

"Yeah." Jack said. "Of course."

Sarah finally pulled back her hands and reached into her pocket. Pulling out a pad and pen, she wrote her phone number on a slip and tore it off the pad, folded it, and handed it through the bars to Jack.

"I have a feeling you're not going to be in here long." She said, drawing a square in the air with her fingers. "Call me if you need anything. Any time." She said with a smile.

Sarah stepped away and headed toward the cellblock door.

"Sarah." Jack said. "Thanks. Really. Thank you for coming to check on me."

"See you tomorrow, Jack." Sarah said, leaving the cell block, hoping she had given Jack some hope, and also hoping it wasn't false hope herself.

CHAPTER THIRTY-THREE

THE NEXT MORNING, after a delicious egg and piece of dry toast that was partially burned and a cold cup of coffee, they escorted me from my cell and back to the interrogation room.

I sat there for a long time. It seemed longer. It was almost infuriating why they brought me to the interview room and left me there for so long, but I was in no position to complain, though I wanted to. It was just in my nature.

I was just getting comfortable in my stainless steel, cold, hard chair when Tuttle came into the room. He had some folders and papers with him. I tried to see what was on the papers, but he flipped them over when he saw what I was doing.

Tuttle sat across from me in the other steel chair that looked every bit as comfortable as the one I was sitting in. I was about to ask Tuttle if he found the cold of the seat and the stiff back was as enjoyable to him as it was to me, or did he prefer sitting on jagged rocks? Then I thought better of it.

Instead, I just looked back at Tuttle, him looking back at me. I was about to scream because of the not knowing what was going to be said or done.

Just then, a knock on the door to the interrogation room broke the tension. I looked at the door and back to Tuttle, who never broke his stare. After a moment that felt like a year, Tuttle got up and went to the door. The officer outside the door said something to him and handed over a folder. Tuttle came back into the room and sat down at the table again.

"Jack," Tuttle said, low and slow. "What did you say to Todd, and what did he say to you?"

My jaw dropped, and I looked at the ceiling for a moment,

trying to remember anything that was said at Todd's apartment. I was such a nervous wreck I couldn't think of anything. Then it hit me.

"The president of the University! Todd said that the president and Clark would argue in her office a lot." I said.

I didn't know if it meant anything, but all I knew was I wanted out of the hot seat, and if this tiny morsel of a memory could help with that goal, all the better.

"Well, that's something. We'll have to look into president Kinzel again." Tuttle said, seeming contemplative. He also seemed less aggressive today.

"Uh, are we done here Tuttle?" I asked, almost pleading. "It's almost time for lunch. I think we're having pickle loaf on Wonderbread today."

"Huh? Oh, yeah. That was a uniform showing me the traffic camera pics of you at the red light near your shop around the time Todd had been murdered." Tuttle said, while waving the folder in his hand toward the door.

"Oh, thank God!" I said, sounding vaguely like I was being told I never had to pay taxes again.

Tuttle ran his hand over his jawline and started thinking out loud. "So, what I'm wondering is this, if you didn't kill Todd, and obviously someone did, who was it and were they the one that called in the tip that you were at Monday's apartment? And why would they specifically target you as a scapegoat?"

"I'd like to know that myself!" I said, probably a little too loudly.

"Yeah. Sorry about the mess, Jack. I really am." Tuttle said. "I hope you know it was just procedure. It's my job. I kept thinking about what you said about that letter. The one saying Todd was innocent? It occurred to me that it may have had no other purpose than to make you look like you were trying to deflect. Someone must have assumed you'd bring that letter in, and that it would seem awfully suspicious after you'd been to Todd's place and then he was found dead. Like I said, sorry for the headache, but, procedure."

139

"Dude! No worries! I'm just happy I don't have to sleep in that cell another night." I said.

"Well, I'm glad of that myself, but I have my work cut out for me now with two murders." Tuttle said flatly. "I'm going to be slammed with paperwork, too."

"Well, if I can help you, I'm always available." I told him.

Tuttle looked at me with a raised brow. "Why didn't you become a cop? If you're so interested in this stuff, it seems like it would be right up your alley."

"Well, during this whole thing, I have been extremely interested in the twists of the case so far, but my first love is music. I couldn't walk away from it. I was twelve when my mother bought me my first electric guitar. It was a cheap piece of junk, but to me it was as exciting as getting a new Les Paul. It made me feel like I was one of my guitar-god idols. I was hooked." I said wistfully.

"Well, if you ever decide to change careers, you have the passion in you, that's for sure." Tuttle said.

"I thought so." I said.

"What do you mean?" Tuttle asked.

"Nothing." I said. I wasn't about to tell Tuttle about my probably now nixed plans for private investigation studies. He would probably try to talk me down, or worse, laugh at me. I felt like he was more of an official cop or nothing kind of guy and might think a P.I. was not as good as an official, died in the wool police detective. Instead, I simply shrugged my shoulders and rolled my eyes to the side. Tuttle looked at me with a suspicious eye, but he didn't ask any further questions, so I looked at it as a close call successfully evaded.

"Listen, I will admit that I am interested in the investigation of this case, and I may want to do it more in the future, but I want to do it on my own terms. I don't think becoming a police officer is the right fit for me, but thanks for the pep talk. I mean it. I appreciate that you feel I could do this." I said while shrugging and looking down, humbled that a police detective, one I admittedly admired, had given me the mark of approval in my potential talent as an investigator.

"No problem, Jack." Tuttle replied. "If you change your mind, let me know. I might be able to pull some strings. Now let's get a burger. I'm starved! Or if you'd rather have the pickle loaf sandwich...?"

I smiled and agreed silently with a nod, and we got up from the desk and headed out.

After some paperwork and getting my belongings back in a manilla envelope, we got in Tuttle's old car and started out for that burger.

Pulling some strings. Someone had pulled some strings to get Todd Monday in the spotlight of this investigation, but when he was killed, it was most likely because it was getting harder to cover the real killer's tracks, as well as keeping Todd the prime suspect. Something wasn't adding up. There had to be some reason that everything pointed to Todd initially. I looked on my phone at my notes I'd been taking while trying not to watch Tuttle's driving. Review was a good distraction. I looked back over the rental agreement Todd signed for the storage unit. Something was nagging at me about it. And then something struck me, but I wasn't sure if it was a real clue or just me getting jittery from hunger. My burned toast and cold coffee weren't holding.

I decided to think about it later. I needed bacon on that burger!

CHAPTER THIRTY-FOUR

A FULL DAY had passed, allowing me to sleep in my own bed for a few hours, and then check on my shop. After checking in a few orders of drum heads and some effects pedals, I had finally found the sweet time to go home, take a hot shower, without being in full view of officers and other inmates, and to climb into my bed for a full nights sleep.

Crud.

I couldn't sleep.

Maybe I was missing my hard, steel jail bed. No. It was this craziness and insanity going on all around me. First the Bösendorfer, then Dr. Clark's murder, and now Todd Monday was dead, and, at least for a day, I went to jail for it! The thought that, even with all that had been done, we were still no closer to finding the killer of Dr. Clark or the thief that took the piano for that matter, was driving me nuts!

By morning, between the lack of sleep and the unending spinning of the gears in my mind trying to figure out this mystery, my head was pounding like a jackhammer. I reached to my bedside stand and ripped open a headache powder. Michelle said I took too many of these things, but then I always had a lot of headaches. Not sure why, but that was just the way it was. And it was awful.

As I washed it down with a gulp of flat soda left out overnight on my nightstand, I began to think about what it could be that we were missing. And how nasty flat soda was.

As much as my head was hurting, my frustration with not being able to figure this conundrum out hurt even more. How many times would we get it wrong before we finally got it right?

I made a mental note to call Tuttle this afternoon and find out if he'd uncovered any new clues.

But now it was time for breakfast. I was in a pancakes kind of mood. The big question was, did I want to make pancakes myself, or just go somewhere? Let's see, I don't have any pancake mix. I also don't have any syrup. Or butter. In fact, the only thing in my fridge was some cheese slices, cold cuts, an aging loaf of bread, and half of an old beer. IHOP it was!

After filling up on a delicious scramble and New York Cheesecake pancakes, and more coffee than most people should consume in a week, I was ready to face the day. I had to admit, there was something that was still bothering me about being away from the shop so much lately. I might have to hire a little help. I mused for a moment about hiring Andrea Keller. It would seem that she is unemployed after all, and now she could work alongside me, her favorite person.

I chuckled to myself.

I knew Andrea Keller would want to come to work for me about as much as the Road Runner would want to work for Wile E. Coyote.

After momentarily thinking about the prospect of roaming around town on a pair of ACME rocket-powered roller skates, I paid my tab and took a last sip of my coffee and then took my leave.

Michelle always told me I drank too much coffee. I protested that there was no such a thing as "too much coffee". She thought it might be the source of my headaches, and she was probably right, but the thought of giving up my java was more painful than the headaches. But here I was again, thinking about Michelle.

It was probably a good twenty minutes that had passed when I realized I was still sitting in the IHOP parking lot with my car running, having drifted away into a string of memories about Michelle and I having breakfast in the mountains, hiking and talking about the future.

The future we were *supposed* to have.

I wiped the tears from my eyes, took a deep breath and backed out of my parking space and headed back to reality.

The entire day was ahead of me and I needed to figure some things out. Namely, why someone wanted to make me the target of the investigation of Todd Monday's murder. Was it just convenient to them that I had gone to see him that day, or did someone have it out for me personally?

I'd never had to ponder things this heavy before, and I have to admit, I didn't like it. I'd be lying to say that I didn't get at least a small thrill from the danger, though. I felt sort of like I was in a thriller movie, just waiting for the next plot twist.

In my case, however, I was pretty tired of plot twists involving me. I wanted smooth sailing now, but I wasn't certain that fate was done with me yet. I was afraid that whoever tried to send me up the river for Monday's murder might not take this minor setback lightly and come at me more directly.

I needed more coffee.

CHAPTER THIRTY-FIVE

THE FACT THAT I was being targeted by someone who had wanted to pin the murder of Todd Monday on me was a little more than disconcerting. It was *outright* disconcerting. Maybe even insanely disconcerting.

I needed to occupy my time and my mind, so I decided it was finally time to hire the help I so desperately needed for the shop. I had been out of the shop more than I'd been in lately, so it was finally time to do something about it.

I logged into my account for advertisers in the local paper to see who all had applied for the job I had posted the other day.

I know. The local paper, right? Well, we're a small town. We still enjoy getting our little rag.

The first applicant I received from the classified ad was one Miranda Artweller. Her application was impressive in that she knew music, instruments, and was a "people person".

Next up was... I looked a few times to see if I was missing something or was not using the website properly. Nope. That was it.

So Miranda Artweller it was.

I called the number on the screen and asked for Miranda. When she answered the phone, I immediately began talking.

"Congratulations! After reviewing a long list of applications and taking a great deal of time to reflect on the pros and cons of each candidate, you were selected to be the new assistant manager of Jack's Music Store!" I said brightly.

The silence on the other end was deafening.

After a few moments that seemed like days, I heard a low, disinterested voice say "Great."

"Uh, well, okay. Um, why don't you come in tomorrow afternoon around two and we'll fill out the paperwork?" I said.

"Okay. I'll be there." She said and hung up.

I looked back at the computer screen and squinted at the line "people person". Yup! That's what it said.

While I was still examining the line on the computer screen, Trevor came into the store.

"Hey, Dad! How's stuff?" Trevor said, skipping down the stairs like he did when he was a kid.

"Stuff is better," I said. "Better than being arrested."

"Wait. Back that up a bit. Arrested?!?" Trevor looked immediately in shock.

"Yup! I was arrested. And by Tuttle, no less!" I replied.

Trevor just looked stunned. Finally, he broke his silence. "Why were you arrested?"

After telling Trevor the whole story about what happened to me, including my arrest and eventual freedom, he was as stunned as he was relieved.

"So, what brings you by, son?" I asked, changing the subject to something that didn't remind me that there was someone who was trying to frame me for murder the day before.

"Oh, well, I was in the neighborhood and thought I would show you something that I found." Trevor pulled a photograph from his messenger bag. I took the photo and saw a family. My family. Me, Michelle, and Trevor when he was about three years old. It was the most beautiful thing I'd ever seen.

"Thank you, son. I didn't even know this still existed. I thought it was lost years ago in a move." I said.

"Yeah, well, I wanted to get it to you. You know, I could get it framed for you really nice. I know a guy." Trevor offered.

"No. I'll take care of it. Thanks, though."

I took the photo and propped it up on the counter in open view.

"Son, I will get this framed and hang it this afternoon. Thank you. Truly." I said. And I meant it. I was intent to put this picture up in a place of prominence.

I turned back to Trevor and smiled warmly. He smiled back and looked at the picture again. "I miss mom." He said.

"Me too." I said. "Me too."

CHAPTER THIRTY-SIX

AS TREVOR AND I were preparing to close the shop and go to an early dinner, I got a call from Tuttle. "I had forensics go back over the crime scene at Todd's apartment and they found something interesting that I thought you might want to know." He said.

"When the forensics team made their secondary sweep, they expanded it to include the posts that held up the awning over the door to Todd Monday's apartment. They got a print." Said Tuttle.

I audibly gasped out loud.

"Get outta town! Well? Tell me! Who's print??" I pleaded.

"Andrea Keller," Tuttle said with a slight hint of giddiness in his voice.

We probably sounded like a couple of gossiping teenage girls to my son, who was looking totally befuddled.

Trevor made a face at me as if to say *enlighten me, please*.

"Tuttle, I'm having dinner with my son and then I'll come by the station. You can show me in person." I said. "I knew that the Keller girl was odd," I added.

"Sure, enjoy your dinner. I feel like this case is coming to a close." Tuttle said.

Trevor and I headed out to dinner with me, feeling like we were really going to close this case. Excited to be a part of it. Hungry, because I had skipped lunch.

We were going to Rubio's Italian, a restaurant I used to take Trevor to when he was little for special occasions. The special occasions being the finding of the precious photo, and now the closing in on the most probable killer of Monday and Clark.

On the way to Rubio's, I let Trevor in on what all had

happened up till now on the case and asked what his thoughts were.

And getting a big break from who killed Todd, and possibly Dr. Clark, counted as a special occasion, no doubt.

"Well, has anyone thought about checking out the background of this girl?" He asked.

"You know, I guess I always assumed the police did that." I said, feeling a little like I had just been accused of being stupid. "Well, I'm sure they will now."

"Is there any way *you* can find out anything?" Trevor pressed.

"Well, I am a little friendly with the lady Desk Sergeant at the precinct. Maybe she could help. I wouldn't want Tuttle to think I was interfering." I noted.

"You? Getting overly involved in something you probably shouldn't? Never!" Trevor said, his words dripping with sarcasm.

"Okay, now. No need to get smart, young man." I said with a smirk.

"And besides all that," Trevor added, spinning his head towards me, "who is this lady Desk Sergeant you were talking about? Anything I should know about? Should I be calling ahead before I visit now, or do you want to just put a sock on the doorknob of the house, like college kids?" Trevor teased.

"Oh, God! Nothing like that!" I said.

"... Not yet, anyway." I added sheepishly.

"I knew it! Dad's got a girlfriend!" Trevor said, doing a little dance move in the car seat. I drove over some railroad tracks a little too fast and let him hit his head on the ceiling of the car, possibly on purpose, but no evidence exists so I will retain my 5th amendment rights.

"Ow." Trevor said, rubbing the newly sore spot on the top of his head. I continued driving to the restaurant with a slight grin on my face. Things in my life were finally beginning to fall into place, but I wasn't sure if I was ready for dating or a relationship.

"I don't know if I'm ready to move on." I said.

"Dad, it's been six years. It's okay for you to move on. Mom wouldn't want you sitting around the music store alone all the time." Trevor said.

"I'm not alone all the time. In fact, I just hired a new employee today." I said, sounding proud of myself.

"Okay, who is she and what does she look like?" Trevor asked suspiciously.

"Oh, well, you see, I haven't exactly met her in person yet so I'm not sure what she looks like, but her name is Miranda Artweller." I said.

"Ahem. Well, I think that's cool. You need to be able to get out of that shop from time to time. Ever since mom died, you've stayed holed up in the shop. You hardly ever do anything for yourself. I think that your new adventures with detective Tuttle have been the first thing you've done outside this shop in quite a while. In fact, I'd say that he's the closest thing to a friend you've had for quite some time." Trevor said. And he was right, I'm ashamed to say. I guess I hadn't realized how reclusive I'd been since Michelle passed. And there it was, laid out before me like a rotten meal, and now I had to eat it.

"You know what? You're right. I've been kind of walled up since your mom died. I just wasn't sure I was ready to move on. I'm still not sure. But I suppose I should try to rejoin the human race and not be a hermit the rest of my life." I said, as much to myself as to Trevor.

Trevor just nodded and looked down at his lap. I could tell there was a part of him that was having trouble getting over his mother's death as well. Maybe my moving on and trying to date again would be therapeutic for both of us. A sort of reset.

When we finally arrived at Rubio's, I turned off the car and we took a moment to gather ourselves and get ready to enjoy a really good meal. I could smell the sauces in the air already. Marinara and Alfredo sent my nose into an uproar. I was salivating at the thought of a juicy meatball and heaping piles of pasta. I was thinking of getting a sweet red wine and topping it off with cheese cake and cherry compote on top.

It was obvious I was ready to eat. Trevor was too. He was wide eyed and grinning ear to ear by the time we got to the doors. We gave each other a look that we both knew all too well. It was the look that meant we were in for an excellent meal and a great time.

I rose my fist for a hearty fist bump and Trevor met it with a solid pop.

As we opened the doors, we were greeted like old friends and served like kings. We had a fantastic meal, enjoyed some laughs, and I had a chance to relax with my son.

It was a good day, but I was eager to get to the station and see what Tuttle had to show me.

CHAPTER THIRTY-SEVEN

WHEN I ARRIVED at the police station, the whole place was in a commotion. I stepped up to the desk and was looking for Desk Sergeant Sarah Laney, but found the desk occupied by an elderly fellow who looked more likely to be employed at Walmart as a greeter than a police department.

"Looking for somebody, Jack?" Came a voice from the door to the left of the desk, opposite the hallway that leads to the interrogation rooms.

I looked in the direction that the voice came from and saw Sarah, dressed in plain clothes, her hair down in long, red waves, and smiling with a sparkle in her eye that made me smile right back despite myself.

"Well, as a matter of fact, I was hoping I'd catch you before you left." I said, sounding a little nervous.

"Oh, really? Well, you just caught me before I left for the night. What exactly did you need, Jack?" she asked with a knowing look.

"I, er, well, actually…" I closed my eyes and exhaled. I gathered my wits and finally spit out the question I wanted to ask. "I was wondering if you would like to get dinner sometime?" I said, feeling like a school boy asking a girl out for the first time. And in some ways, it was the same. It was the first time I'd asked a woman out since the before I met Michelle.

I was holding my breath in anticipation. She looked like she was trying to decide whether to have chocolate or vanilla. I was dying inside.

"Well… what did you have in mind?" she said, finally.

"How do you feel about Italian food? Rubio's is a favorite of mine, and I think it will be for you, too." I asked her. I was sort of surprised I said it as smoothly as I did because the reality was that I was terrified at that moment, and I realized that I had not put a single thought into what I would say if she seemed interested. And she did. She was obviously open to going out with me. And I was excited by that. I was actually about to jump out of my socks. I was so excited! It surprised me that I was able to ask her out and not look like an idiot in the process.

"I love Italian!" Sarah said, looking genuinely excited now.

"Great! Why don't you come by the shop tomorrow and we'll nail down the details?" I asked, clasping my hands together so she couldn't see how clammy they were getting, or how badly they were shaking.

Sarah dropped her gaze down to her feet and laughed a little, adorable laugh. "Okay, sounds good."

"Good!" I said. "See you tomorrow then?"

"Yeah. See you tomorrow." Sarah said and turned on her heel to go back in the door she had just come out of. She stopped and laughed out loud.

"Oh! I was leaving, wasn't I?" Sarah said as she rolled her eyes and cocked a goofy smile. It just made me melt.

Sarah pulled her bag up over her shoulder by the strap and quickly headed for the door.

I just stood there in silence, watching the door slowly come to a close as the hydraulic hissed.

"Get a room." Came a voice from behind me. I turned to see that the elderly gentleman that was the night shift Desk Sergeant had bore witness to the entire awkward exchange. His eyebrow was raised, and he looked unamused. I chose to ignore his comment and keep things professional.

"Detective Tuttle, please. He's expecting me." I said.

"Mm-hmm." He grunted as he picked up the phone and called back to Tuttle's desk.

Within a few moments, I was greeted by Tuttle, who looked like he was excited to show me the fresh evidence. We headed back to Tuttle's desk, and he pulled a chair from another desk over for me to sit in. Tuttle mussed about the papers on his desk in an attempt to make it seem tidier, but was unsuccessful in his endeavor. After a few moments of him trying to make some semblance of a difference in the travesty of a desk, he finally gave up and pulled a folder from a drawer on his side of the desk and slapped it on the top of the desk across the papers that were already there.

"Take a look." He said with a proud and excited look on his face.

I pulled the folder over to me with two fingers and flipped the front cover open with my other hand. I don't claim to be any kind of genius when it comes to forensic information, but one thing was obvious. A positive match on the fingerprint of Andrea Keller. Her profile was in the folder as well.

The history that this girl had with a young woman in her high school was like something from a movie. *Single White Female* comes to mind, with just a little *Fatal Attraction* in the mix for good measure.

The file read that Andrea Keller had been questioned by the police in an incident that occurred in her hometown when she was in high school. It seems that her friend had been attacked and ended up in the hospital. Andrea was brought in by the local police to be questioned about the incident and it was eventually disclosed that Andrea had confronted her friend a few months before the assault over a disagreement over a boy. And before that, it was said that Andrea had been almost obsessive of the girl. The police felt that Andrea was a little too "on the nose" about some of the details surrounding her friend's attack, though they couldn't necessarily place her at the scene, and the girl never got a good look at her assailant.

At any rate, I could see where Tuttle was going with this. His excitement was infectious. It certainly made sense that Andrea Keller was our killer. Her steely glares, her obvious disliking of Todd Monday. Her darn near homicidal history. The idea then crossed my mind that if she killed Monday, then what if she was connected with the killing of Dr. Clark? I asked Tuttle about it, and he replied with a shrug.

"Nothing solid yet, but if she ever crossed paths with Clark, we're going to find out. I have some uniformed officers canvasing the campus and asking questions. If anyone knows about anything, then we're going to find out. I'm also having forensics go back over the evidence to look for Keller's prints again. This is the best lead we've had." He paused for a second, then added, "I'm not going to let her get away with this."

CHAPTER THIRTY-EIGHT

THE NEXT DAY, I decided I was going to have to find out what happened to the girl that Keller was obsessed with back in her hometown. The reports we looked at in the police dossier on Andrea certainly made me worry about what happened to the girl.

After looking into the subject a little, I found out that a criminal record isn't always sealed after a minor turns 18. Especially when it was a violent crime. And the attack by Andrea Keller on one Lisa Stone was certainly a violent one. It made the papers. At least it made the only newspaper I was able to find for Andrea's hometown. Online research, as it turns out, is actually more than watching YouTube videos about making the perfect buttermilk biscuits.

During all of this, in all this craziness that was going on around me, my plans on working towards becoming a private investigator had been dashed. I still couldn't believe I was thinking about going back to school on a lark. I was, however, more interested in seeing what I could learn from Tuttle. I was never a spectacular student, at least when I was younger. Although, it seemed that in my having lived a little bit of life to this point, I had somewhere along the way become more attentive, and a more apt student. Who knew?

I saw hanging out with Tuttle during this investigation as a learning experience in itself. I wouldn't be donning a cap and gown and accepting a rolled and ribboned piece of parchment from an esteemed faculty member at the end of this program, but it would prepare me to take on the next interesting case that popped up on the nightly news. Even if only so I could more ably assist the best detective in the Harrow's Gate Police Department. In fact, I was hoping that I could work with a certain grumpy detective in the future, if only he would be receptive to such a thing.

Tuttle certainly fit the bill for a mentor. He had been a working detective for many years now, and we already had a rapport. In fact, I was actually excited to see what nuggets of wisdom Tuttle would bestow upon me. He seemed to always know what to do next. I get moments of inspiration, but Tuttle usually always has a plan.

The newspaper article referring to the incident with Andrea Keller and Lisa Stone explained that, though the Stone girl hadn't seen who attacked her, forensic evidence concluded that Andrea had been the attacker, and that she had tried to convince Stone that someone else had done it. The article closed neatly, stating that Andrea Keller had been charged with attempted manslaughter.

I started wondering, was Andrea Keller at the center of all of this craziness with her apparent history of violence, and just seemingly outright insanity? Plus, she was mean to me.

Okay, maybe I was venting a little on that one, but it was quite obvious that the girl was a little troubled. If she was after this Stone girl and did what she did to her, it might be possible that she was pulling the poor Baylor girl around as well. I remembered the look on Autumn Baylor's face that day as they were leaving the coffee shop. Maybe her look was actually a cry for help. If Andrea is helicoptering around her all the time, Autumn may not be able to escape her influence.

I dug a little deeper. The local police had gone on record in the town newspaper stating that they were able to find sufficient evidence to push forward on the attempted manslaughter charges and tack on attempted murder, though it appeared that nothing ever came of it due to procedural issues.

Before I went so far as to declare that it was Andrea Keller in the library with the candlestick I wanted to find out more about the girl in the article, but first I had a date with another girl, the girl I spoke to on the phone about the position at my store. She seemed less than excited on the phone, but maybe she would seem more bubbly in person. At any rate, I was going to need someone to man the shop while I'm finishing my classes and when I hopefully get to shadow Tuttle. The first step was done. I just needed to meet the newly hired help in person.

CHAPTER THIRTY-NINE

I APPROACHED THE door to Jack's Music and sat my fresh coffee down on the pavement just to the left of my foot. I could smell the nutty aroma of the coffee drifting up to my nose as I turned the key in the cylinder and heard the mechanism of the lock fall into place. After flipping the open sign over and heading down the stairs, I realized I had forgotten my coffee outside the door.

As I headed back up the stairs I was stopped in my tracks by a young lady in black Chucks and black jeans, a black-and-white striped long-sleeved shirt and long black hair surrounding a pretty, but pale, face that didn't appear to have seen much sun in the last few years. She was holding my coffee.

"Uh, well, thank you." I said, taking the coffee from the girl's hand that was adorned with several stainless steel rings, one carved into a skull, and another one in the sculpture of a snake, wrapped around the finger. "Can I help you find an instrument?" I asked hopefully.

"Uh, no. I'm here for the job." She said.

"Oh! Sorry. I thought you were here to buy something. Actually, I'm sorry, but the job has already been filled. I hired someone yesterday. A real people person." I ground my teeth on the last part.

"I'm Miranda Artweller. You're talking about me." She said.

I admittedly took a beat to take it all in. Miranda Artweller was a cross between Wednesday Addams and Chris Angel. Of course, I also realized I am not getting any younger and the folks my age thought I looked creepy when I was her age just because I had long hair at the time and wore a lot of metal bands' logos on my shirts. She deserved a chance. Also, I had already hired her.

"Oh, sorry! I had no idea what you looked like. I mean, I didn't know what I was looking at. I mean, oh lord, I was not expecting you until later, I guess." I said. I sounded like an idiot.

"Oh, yeah. Well, I really need this job I guess, and I thought maybe I could start today." She said.

I wasn't sure I could do that. I don't even know if she could run the register. All I knew was that I needed help, and help, dark and solemn as it was, was here. Like getting Batman when you were expecting Wonder Woman.

At any rate, I led her around the counter and started to show her the point of sale system on the computer. She immediately demonstrated that she was already quite comfortable on the system by quickly tapping a few times on the screen and stopping on the screen used to add a new user to the system. I was both impressed and relieved. At least I knew I didn't have to teach her how to ring up sales, apparently.

"I see you're comfortable in this system?" I asked.

"Oh, yeah. My uncle has a jewelry shop in Dallas, and he has the same system. I worked there for a summer about two years ago." She said. I was also excited to hear she was apparently used to selling high-ticket items. It's one thing to talk to someone about why they need to buy a $25 toaster, it's another to successfully explain to someone about the benefits of a $2,000 broach, or in this case, a guitar. Maybe a sweet, made in the U.S.A. Fender Stratocaster.

I showed Miranda around the store and the stockroom in the back, the two soundproof rooms for music lessons, and finally I introduced her to Sheila Bryant upstairs.

After we headed back down to the shop, we heard the bells on the door ring and a woman and a boy who looked to be around fifteen or sixteen came down the stairs.

"Welcome to Jack's Music." I said cheerfully. The mom smiled and nodded. The boy didn't acknowledge. I approached the two, with Miranda following close behind. And that's when it hit me. I decided to throw Miranda in the deep end and see exactly what she could do. I would let her take these folks and see how she worked in a real-world situation. Of course, I would step in if it all went haywire, but I wanted to see how comfortable she was under pressure.

"My assistant manager, Miranda, will help you find something." I said and looked to see if Miranda was panicking. She wasn't. In fact, she seemed like she wanted to say "It's about time".

"Oh, thank you. My name is Lucille Brandt." The lady said, her hand extended to Miranda. Miranda gave offered her hand in return and presented a firm handshake.

"Hello ma'am, my name is Miranda, like Mr. Gulley said. So what kind of guitar were you looking for today?" Miranda said, exposing a straightforward, no-nonsense side that would bode well in a sales career.

"And whom is the instrument for, may I ask?" she said.

"Oh, it's for my son, Josh. He wants to learn to play," the woman said, nodding towards her son, who was looking at a guitar that was way more than he probably needs if he was just beginning.

"Okay, fantastic!" Miranda said, sounding genuinely excited. She turned to face Josh and stepped toward him one step. "So what kind of music will you be playing?" She asked, narrowing her eyes in concentration.

"Uh, well, I want to play metal, I guess." Josh said, mustering up all the meal bravado he could channel from Dave Mustaine.

"Ah, metal. What kind of tone are you looking for? Hair metal, thrash? Maybe Death?" Miranda asked Josh in earnest.

"Death?" Lucille asked, seeming both shocked and confused.

"It's a kind of metal, mom." Josh said, rolling his eyes. Lucille did not look amused. *Don't let the kid lose the decision maker for you, Miranda,* I thought.

"I know. The name is supposed to elicit the same kind of reaction your parents probably had when they first heard Black Sabbath playing on your turntable. But now Sabbath seems pretty pedestrian by comparison. Just an evolution of the same kind of musical rebellion." Miranda added, touching a nostalgia nerve in mom, as well as getting a knowing nod and subtle grin in return. Back on the hook. Not bad.

"Uh, well, not death. I'm not that angst-ridden. Yet." Josh said and smiled, looking like he had just told a great joke. We all chuckled politely.

"Actually, I like a heavy sound with a nice high end for shredding." Josh said.

"Hmm, okay..." Miranda began looking around the room and stopped her eyes on a Dean guitar. A Dave Mustaine signature model, the VMNT. "I think I see just the thing." Miranda said and headed for the guitar.

While I had a couple of different ones with various paint schemes and album art, Miranda grabbed a stock black one. Not bad for a beginner. Or anyone. Miranda picked up the guitar and put a strap that was lying on the amplifier next to it on the strap pegs and slid the guitar strap over Josh's head and over his shoulder, adjusting the strap so the guitar would hang just right in front of Josh.

"How does that feel?" Maranda asked with a smirk on her face.

"It's heavy." Josh said smiling, running his left hand up and down the neck of the instrument. The clean, V-shaped body was enormous on Josh. I have to admit, it looked good on him. Miranda took a cord and plugged one end into the guitar and the other into a Marshall amp sitting on the floor next to him. She turned on the amplifier and a warm hum came from the speaker. A screech came from the amp as Josh moved his left hand on the neck, scraping the strings with his fingers. Miranda handed him a pick and, to my surprise, placed Josh's fingers into the position to strike a power chord. Then she made a motion like she was strumming a chord on a guitar, clearly indicating that Josh do the same. He did. And it growled.

The warm, gravelly tone of the guitar through the amplifier, along with the built in distortion effect on the amp, created a sound that would make Mustaine proud.

"Oh, yeah!" Josh said. Obviously exhilarated, Josh nodded his head, almost ready to start head-banging right away.

"I. Want. It!" Josh said. Mom laughed a little.

"That's the first I've seen him really excited in quite a while." She said. "What else will we need? And don't you do lessons?"

Lucille was speaking my language. Miranda was making an impression, and a good one at that. And I was already thinking about how I could spend my newfound free time.

CHAPTER FORTY

THE BÖSENDORFER SAT covered on a truck parked in the evidence's rear lockup where the harsh overhead dome lamps cast a blueish white light down on the piano and the surrounding shelves full of various bagged, tagged, and boxed evidence of multitudes of crimes.

Officer Conner Garrison opened the door to the evidence lockup and started looking through boxes for bags that contained 9mm slugs that were needed for a courtroom presentation in the morning.

Garrison pulled a box from a shelf with a large W on the side and sat it on the table in the middle of the room. He took the lid off of the box and flipped through the dividers until he finally stopped on a tab labeled "Wells". He pulled out a small, discreet baggie and put the lid back on the box before lifting the box and sliding it back onto the shelf.

Just as Garrison put the box back on the shelf, he heard something.

He stopped, looking over his shoulder and holding still and silent. *What was that?* He thought. *I bet a rat. I hate rats.*

Garrison pulled his Freeze+P pepper spray off his belt and started slowly looking around the shelves. The overhead lights unfortunately cast hard shadows in the corners of the room, making it hard to see there, also making for perfect hiding spots for the rats he was searching for.

He crept around the corner of the shelves closest to the truck and slowly reached for the box on the bottom shelf, moving it aside for a better view of… nothing.

He scratched his chin and neck, scanning the area for any

sight of what could have made the noise. Whatever it had been, it seemed to be gone now.

Garrison holstered his can of Freeze+P back on his belt and quickly forgot about searching for rats or whatever it was.

The lid to the evidence box had fallen on the floor, so Garrison leaned over to pick it up. As he stood back up, the pain was sudden and his vision went out first with what seemed like a flash of light and then darkening to a single point, like an old television set being turned off.

The cold on Garrisons' face was the first thing he noticed. Then the pain of his tailbone. Curious feeling. Never paid much attention to it before. Hurts like heck, though.

Then his head signaled. The headache was like a migraine, almost enough to make him puke. He was still seeing stars. The cold on his face was the cool cement floor of the evidence lockup. He could see a little better now, but he realized he'd been knocked out. Were they still here? He wanted to reach for his weapon, but immediately realized his cuffs had been put on his own wrists.

Garrison managed to stumble to his feet, but the blow to his head was making it hard to stand straight. He leaned into the wall closest to him. The realization that he could smell air, like the outside, got him to look at the bay door. He looked up and saw dozens of gnats and a moth or two darting around the hanging lights overhead. Garrison realized that the bay door to the outside was open, letting bugs in the building.

The ringing that had been in his ears since he woke was starting to subside, only to be replaced by another. The station alarm was almost deafening. Garrison noticed the keys to the truck weren't on the hook on the wall. The truck was gone, too.

It took less than an instant for it to register with Garrison that if the truck was gone, so too was the Bösendorfer.

Garrison managed to hit the door handle well enough to exit the storage area and make his way down the hall to The Hole.

"RAINES!" Garrison yelled. "RAINES!!"

Linda Raines emerged from the door labeled Medical Examiner and gasped audibly before rushing to Garrison and helping him to a bench in the hallway, where she immediately started checking him for wounds.

"What the heck happened?!? Oh, God, honey! You're bleeding!" Raines exclaimed as she began pulling whatever alcohol swabs she had in her coat pockets, tearing them open to clean the wound.

"Somebody knocked me out long enough to cuff me and drive the truck with the piano out of the bay." Garrison said while nursing the mother of all headaches. "Call the captain and Tuttle, too I guess."

"I need to clean you up and get you to a hospital. I'm equipped to help folks who are already beyond help here, not you. I'll call upstairs and then we're going to the emergency room." Raines said, making sure Garrison understood that this was in no uncertain terms.

On the ride to the hospital, Raines kept glancing at Garrison's pump knot on the back of his head. She thought to herself, *he's lucky he woke up from this.*

"Did you see them? Can you remember any details about them?" She asked, trying to gather any clues as to the identity of Garrison's attacker.

"I don't remember seeing anything. I heard something. Looked around. Thought it was rats. I gave up looking and, bam. Whoever it was got me." Garrison said while wincing and trying not to give in to the sleepiness that was trying to overtake him. He realized he probably had a concussion and needed to stay conscious until he got to the hospital.

"Stay with me, Connor. Tell me about what you were doing in there. What did you need from evidence?" Raines asked, attempting to keep Garrison talking so he wouldn't pass out.

After reaching the hospital, Linda Raines got help from an orderly getting Garrison into the emergency room. Linda stayed in the ambulance bay and tried to compose herself before heading back to the station.

Linda's phone started buzzing. It was Tuttle.

"How's Garrison, Linda?" Tuttle asked.

"He took a pretty good knock to his noggin, Mark. I haven't heard anything yet. They just took him in." She said. "Somebody got the piano. Took the truck and all."

"Yeah, dammit. I know. How did they even get in there?" Tuttle said.

"I don't know, but you gotta find this guy, Mark." Linda said. "Somebody that bold is not going to stop at that. I'm afraid there's more to come if you don't end this soon."

CHAPTER FORTY-ONE

THE TRUCK CONTAINING the Bösendorfer drove straight through the gate of the impound lot, snapping the latch on the fence, careened around the corner and down the street. The truck's frame groaned under the strain while the tires screeched out, about to pull away from the rims.

The officer in the guard shack to the impound lot next to the evidence hold scrambled to see who was at the wheel but was unable to see any features.

How did they get in without being seen? Where did they get the keys?

These questions all racing through the guard's mind. As he headed out of the lot and into the street to see if he could get a heading on the truck, he noticed a section of fencing pulled back and a cut of binding wire laying on the ground.

The truck was long gone. The guard ran back to the shack and pulled the alarm, while calling for help over his radio. The officer stated the facts and asked for assistance in the lot. He knew they would have to mark off the area to look for evidence, so he locked the gates down the best he could.

A moment later, Detective Mark Tuttle came over the radio, understandably upset. "What happened?!? How did they get in the gate? What the..." he went on, more venting than asking proper questions. He was too angry.

The guard was sweating now. He would be happy to still have a job after this little fiasco. *I wonder what Florida is like this time of year?* He thought. The realization set in that he may be taking an unpaid vacation soon, and not because he wanted to.

Tuttle slammed his hand on the steering wheel of his Cadillac, then screamed a short, guttural yell. He ran his hands over his head to smooth his hair after his short outburst and took a deep, cleansing breath.

He was understandably upset, but at this point, he couldn't change that. He had to accept it, and start doing anything he could to get the Bösendorfer back safely.

Okay, he thought, *where would someone take the piano that they wouldn't be seen?*

The truth was, put simply, Tuttle had no idea.

This prompted another wheel-slam, shout combo.

I was on the phone with Sarah when she shushed me in the middle of a story about the rock band I used to tour with. I was a little hurt, thinking she was so bored with my story that she ultimately decided to end it prematurely. But then she gasped.

"What is it?" I asked.

"The piano was stolen from the station!" Sarah said in a shocked tone.

"What?!? What do you mean? How could somebody steal a grand piano... from the police?!?" I probably said a little too loudly, almost shouting.

Sarah shushed me again.

"Why do you keep..."

"Shh!"

"Ugh!"

"I'm listening to my work radio." Sarah finally explained.

After a moment of quiet on the phone, she finally broke the silence.

"Okay, the piano was still on the truck they took it to the station on. The perp stole the truck and drove away with the piano." She explained.

I couldn't make sense of it. If the person who stole the truck was the person who stole the piano and presumably murdered Dr. Clark, they should be on the lam. Why would they go to the police station, of all places? And why steal the piano again?

While I was pondering these deep questions, I was startled by the alarm sound on my phone. It was the Emergency Alert System. There was a severe storm warning in effect. I could see through the window that it was getting pretty dark outside already.

I just hoped that whoever had the Bösendorfer was protecting it from the elements.

"Sarah, I'm going to call Tuttle." I said.

"Okay, don't get yourself in trouble." She replied.

This whole thing was becoming stressful to me, even if I didn't really have a dog in that fight, other than a fascination with the procedure and the outcome. If I'm stressed, I can imagine what pressure Tuttle's under.

I wondered what pressure the thief/killer felt. Why did they put the spotlight back on themself by stealing the piano again? Why not just leave town and not look back?

Then something occurred to me.

I wanted to run it by Tuttle.

CHAPTER FORTY-TWO

I HOPPED IN my car and backed out into the street in front of the store. It was still early in the evening, but the sky was getting so dark that most of the shops along the street had turned on their lights and lit their signs. The storm was not far off now, and it was getting even more ominous, with dense cloud cover overhead.

I drove all over town since it was a small community, and there was little chance you could miss a truck with a priceless Bösendorfer just casually cruising around the city.

I dialed Tuttle's number, and it went to voicemail. Not sure what I expected. This whole thing just blew up, and it was his case. He's probably stressed out and dealing with a load of calls, so I left a message.

"Tuttle, this is Jack. I was thinking, why would somebody put themselves in even more hot water by stealing the piano a second time? I got thinking about it and it occurred to me that maybe it's because it wasn't for them. Maybe they were stealing it for someone else. I'm making sense out of this mess. Maybe you're coming up with the same conclusions? I'd like to talk to you about it in person. Call me back."

I had no sooner put my phone back in my pocket when it started ringing. Tuttle was calling me back. I slid my finger across the screen of my phone and answered excitedly.

"Tuttle! I heard about the piano being stolen again. Do you remember how Andrea Keller was always hovering over Autumn Baylor? At first I thought Andrea was just being there for her friend, but then I felt like there was something more menacing going on. That's when I also started to think that maybe, just maybe, Andrea was some sort of threat to Autumn. But now I think…" I was almost talking faster than Tuttle could follow. He stopped me.

"Slow down, Jack! What does this have to do with the piano?" He asked.

Tuttle was right. I was rambling. I took a deep, cleansing breath, exhaled, and slowly started again.

"Okay, here's what I'm getting at…" I started.

Just then, Tuttle got a call over his police radio stating that they had reported the piano in a field off State Road 33. Coulton Field. I knew it well. I took Jessica Reynolds up there in high school while we were dating and we would, well… that's beside the point. "Why is the piano at our tiny burg's equivalent to make-out point?" I asked.

"Well, Jack, tell you what, just meet me there and you can tell me. I gotta go." Then Tuttle ended the call.

I hadn't quite processed the fact that the priceless antique piano we had all been searching for was now just dumped off in a field. A field?? Why???

I knew my answers weren't anywhere but in that field.

I sped up and headed towards SR33. I was seeing droplets hit my windshield now. Not good. Not when there was a priceless musical instrument in a freaking field right now!

I stepped on the gas and gripped the wheel a little tighter. I had to get there and try to save the Bösendorfer.

The storms were inevitable now, and the skies were dark; the wind was picking up fast, and you could feel the surrounding energy in the air. Lightning and thunder were soon to arrive.

As I turned up on the scene, I could see the Bösendorfer in all its glory. It stood out like a sore thumb, because how couldn't it? Only a priceless antiquity, just sitting in an open field with a terrible storm on the way. It turned my stomach.

I wasn't close enough yet to make out any details. All I can hope was that no damage had been done. I looked from side to side and all around the field for any trace of anyone lurking nearby. I wanted to approach the piano, but I also didn't want to be taken unaware by some ne'er-do-well.

I wish I could say that I wasn't scared, but the truth is, if a cat had sneezed, I would've wet my pants.

At that very moment, a lightning strike cracked. *Holy mackerel!* I thought. *I think I did! I think I peed a little!*

I really needed to get a hold of myself, so I tried to calm down and get a grip, but it may have been too much to ask. I was even nervously running cliche's in my head, just like that!

I stood back outside the perimeter of the field but wasn't sure what to do next. I certainly didn't want to traipse around a crime scene, potentially destroying evidence. Tuttle would never let me hear the end of that one.

I wished Tuttle were there. He knew the policy and procedure of the situation. All I knew was what I'd seen on crime scene investigation shows on TV. I was pretty sure that I shouldn't rely on the accuracy of a TV script writer under a deadline. At any rate, I'd already spoken with the Tuttle, and I knew he'd be there any minute now.

I looked back out towards the road, scanning for headlights, flashlights, any evidence that Tuttle or any other officers might be on their way.

All I knew was that the storm was getting closer and closer. The wind was really picking up now. I feared what we would lose if the storm hit with the Bösendorfer exposed in this field, but even with my optimism, I knew that my window of opportunity was closing quickly.

I wrung my hands and glanced around the tree line and out towards the road again.

Still no sign of Tuttle, or anyone else, for that matter.

I had to decide then. I could stand here at the field's edge, waiting for a storm to ruin the piano, or head towards it to see if there was any way I could save it, and possibly contaminate a crime scene. And God help me, if there was another body inside that piano, I would lose my mind!

I hoped that the chances of another body being in the piano were quite low, and I assumed that saving what was possibly the largest piece of evidence in a murder investigation that the Harrows Gate Police Department has ever had would be pretty important.

I decided, finally, to start slowly making my way into the field towards the Bösendorfer.

CHAPTER FORTY-THREE

THE WIND HOWLED as the grass whipped around my knees. I could see the Bösendorfer in the middle of the field, intact. Even so, this was no place for such an instrument. It looked like some kind of setup for a music video, but without special care taken for protecting the piano, like a music video production would take, I winced at the beautiful thing sitting in the clearing.

The storm was nearing. It would mean rain soon, and that would mean disaster for the beautiful Bösendorfer. It never should have been brought into this type of circumstances in the first place. I was looking for Andrea in the clearing, but I scanned the tree line, to no avail. I heard a snap in the wooded area to my left and out about 30 yards. It could have been the ever-increasing winds, but then maybe not. If it was Andrea Keller, she was being careless. Wind or a killer, it startled me. The thought occurred to me I was in way over my head.

Where is Tuttle? I wondered, clenching my fists, the moisture in my palms cold sweat, not rain.

I started taking slow, but measured, steps toward the piano. What would I find when I got to it? Another body? I was almost ready to just drop it and head back to my car. Let Tuttle handle it when he and the cops got here. But I couldn't. I knew I had to know. It was like a sickness; I guess. The need.

I thought I heard another crack from the woods, but then it could have been my imagination. Or the wind, which was really quite something now, could have broken a limb on a tree. They were swaying with the wind, like the palm trees you see on the news when the meteorologist, who really shouldn't be out in a hurricane, is reporting that the state of Florida is on high alert and that everyone who hadn't evacuated were recommended to stay indoors. I felt like the meteorologist. Being blown one way, then the next, wondering why I was here myself. Was I crazy? I think that's fully established by now.

In fact, that's what this entire case had been like, a hurricane that blew you from one side to the other, never knowing when it may just flatten you.

Or a piano.

The Bösendorfer was shaking a little now. The lid was bumping up and down as the wind tried to both open the piano and slam it shut. It was as if the storm had multiple personalities which wanted the piano open, yet closed at the same time, like a crazy man on a street corner, arguing with himself.

I had made my way to the piano. I was looking it over for damage. They had moved it off the truck and into this open field, obviously in a hasty manner. Only this time it was not by the semi-careful hands of a professional moving company, but instead by the abusive hands of a lunatic who simply wanted it moved. Here. Into what was essentially a clearing in the woods.

But why?? Even if professional movers moved it, it wouldn't make sense to leave it in the grassy field. I probably had a perplexed look on my face because I just couldn't make heads or tails of it.

I heard the sound of the police sirens blaring in the wind. Tuttle was close, thank God. Maybe he would be able to shed some light on that aspect. The "why here". I was pretty sure I had figured out the who and the why of the murders. But why *this* clearing?

Tuttle was coming across the clearing from approximately the same point I had started from. He would be by my side in just a moment. I started talking in my excitement to explain before he was quite all the way there. I was yelling over the howling winds just so he could hear me.

"The piano will be okay, I think, as long as we get it covered before the rain hits." I said, holding the piano lid down so it didn't pop up and down any more.

"I have uniformed officers grabbing tarps from the station." Tuttle said. He was winded, but I understood. "You said you knew something, Jack. What is it?" Tuttle asked.

"I know who killed Dr. Clark. And I know who stole the piano in the first place. And who killed Todd Monday." I said. Tuttle looked confused.

"Keller. We know it was Keller." Tuttle said.

"Well, she was part of it," I said, "but there's a little more to the story."

Just then there was a loud clap of thunder, almost simultaneously with a blinding flash of lightening.

It shook the ground. We were both shocked, no pun intended.

Just then, while we were both jolted, Andrea Keller came, well, bolting from the woods.

Sorry, I can't help myself.

She had something in her hands. She was screaming like a banshee, which only seemed appropriate as the storm was howling ever more near.

Tuttle reached in his trench coat and pulled out his gun and started to swing the weapon in Andrea's direction, but she met his hand with the tree branch that she was carrying, making a cracking sound that was nearly as loud as the snap that the branch had made only a few minutes before when she broke it off the tree in the woods.

Tuttle's gun flew to the ground about a yard from where we were standing. Both Tuttle and my eyes followed the gun as it went to the ground. That's probably why we missed it when Andrea reared back with the limb and came down over the back of Tuttle's head, knocking him to the ground.

He wasn't moving. I wasn't either, for that matter, but my problem was shock, not a massive blow to the head.

Andrea looked crazed and angry, but a little scared too. Like she wanted to just run away. I wanted her to run away, too. Heck, *I* wanted to run away. But I didn't. I just kept holding that shuttering piano closed. It petrified me that I might be the next one who was going to be dead. But, strangely, I was afraid that no one would know what happened, what *really* happened, even more than being bludgeoned to death with a tree limb.

Okay, that was a lie. I think the being bludgeoned to death really did scare me more, but I digress.

"Why did you keep bothering us?" Andrea screamed. "You aren't a cop! You should have left us alone!"

She made a good point, but that was irrelevant. I had to help put this thing to bed.

I looked over at Tuttle who was now conscious but nursing a broken hand. He couldn't seem to get up. I kept talking to keep Andrea's attention until Tuttle could get his gun, or the officers got back from getting tarps, or just to keep her from killing me.

"It was you that stole the Bösendorfer from Devon Hall, just like you stole the piano from the police evidence unit tonight. But you didn't kill Clark, did you?" I said. Tuttle, who had been nursing the newly acquired pump knot on the back of his head, suddenly looked up and gave me a quizzical look.

"And that would have been the end of it…" Andrea said, quite obviously crying now. The rain was starting now as well, meeting her tears and blending with them as they both began to wet her cheeks.

"You had the moving company come to the University and move the Bösendorfer to the warehouse. The flyers that said there had been a concert by Autumn Baylor that evening were fakes. Fakes made by you. You see, I noticed you were gripping a graphic design text book the day I met you and was asking Autumn questions. I figured, as someone taking graphic design courses, access to design software would be a given for you, and if you were even just a little good at Photoshop, you could have taken any old flyer from one of Autumn's real concerts and changed the dates and passed them off as new ones."

"Shut up!" She yelled and reared back the limb but stopped short of swinging it.

I continued, mostly because it was buying time, but I was also on a roll.

"It was enough to fool the movers into thinking they were simply moving the piano into storage after a concert, wasn't it? But you thought you'd cleaned up all the flyers that were no doubt strewn all over the seats and floor of Devon Hall, but you missed one. And I found it. It didn't seem important at first, but I kept it. It's in my drawer at my shop." I said. "Evidence."

Her house of cards was falling all around her. I could see she was visibly shaken now, and the rain was in full downpour. Any hope of saving the Bösendorfer from the storm was almost nil now. Damn. I finally let go of the lid. I continued to explain.

"And the moving company was something I thought about after seeing a play. I realized that one person couldn't have moved the piano out of the auditorium without help. And the play made that connection for me. A moving company was the next logical conclusion for getting the piano out of the auditorium and into the warehouse."

"Sounds like a stupid play!" Andrea was seething now.

"You have no idea!" I agreed. She was getting tired of listening to me, but she listened. So I kept up the explanation, still trying to buy time for the police to arrive.

"The only question I had was who had a key to the Auditorium that could open it after hours for the movers, but then it occurred to me that Todd Monday could have opened that door for you if you told him it was for Autumn. Because he was in love with her, wasn't he? He would have burned the whole place down for Autumn if she'd only asked. But you told him she wanted to play the Bösendorfer, and he bought it." I was reaching here, but I was trying to keep the limb in Andrea's hand from meeting my skull, so I was keeping it conversational. "You counted on him not telling anyone that you had asked for the doors to be unlocked because you knew that Todd was so scared of Clark that he would never want to confess to having opened the doors on the very night that the Bösendorfer had been stolen. Also, there is the fact that Todd hated Dr. Clark. He probably derived some sort of satisfaction from watching her come apart over the theft of the piano. And when the police arrested him for the murder of Dr. Clark, it all made sense after seeing his violent reaction in Dr. Clark's office. And the affidavit we got from the storage company's secretary seemed to be a nail in the coffin for Todd." I raised my hands a little, partly from reflex, seeing as the girl was wielding a branch that was heavy enough to crack my skull if she were to swing fast enough. "But when I looked at the receipt from the storage unit, I saw that the secretary who signed off on the rental was you. I didn't realize it at first, which is probably what you were hoping because you just used your initials instead of signing. An oversight, I'm sure, but I bet you thought that renting the unit in Todd's name would cast all the suspicion on him. And it did... for a while." I said.

"But there was a problem. The forensics gave every indication that the killer was left-handed, but when I burst into Clark's office in time to see Todd throwing the chair against the wall behind Dr. Clark, I noticed he threw with his right arm. The more I thought about that, the more it bothered me."

I started slowly moving away from Tuttle, trying to get Andrea to come away from him. I was careful not to lose my footing in the softening soil beneath me due to the driving rain.

"I see that you, Andrea, are holding the limb in your left hand." I said.

"I didn't kill Dr. Clark." Andrea said, barely audible through the storm.

"I know." I said. With that, Tuttle scooted himself to a sitting position and the look of confusion on his face told me that he hadn't followed along with me to the same conclusion. Andrea looked confused, and a little concerned as well.

"You see, the medical examiner concluded that the killer was not only left-handed, but that they were shorter than Dr. Clark due to the angle of the blow to her head. Andrea, I noticed that you and Todd Monday were about the same height. Both of you were taller than Clark." I pointed out.

Andrea seemed to have the wind knocked out of her. She obviously knew where I was going now, even if Tuttle was a little lost.

"And there was more. Whoever hit Clark strangled her, too. The M.E. Said that the strangling happened *after* the blow to the head. That was a crime of passion. The killer had a grudge, anger towards her, they were hurt by her... something." I said. "You barely knew Clark. I can't imagine this being that personal to you. Now, Todd Monday was something all together different. Wasn't it?" Andrea went cold. Her face went from anger to an emotional ice block in a split second. It was enough to make me gulp.

"The look I'm sure you gave Todd, right before you killed him." I said, and then the thought that I was now in her crosshairs was sobering. It was getting darker. The lightning was increasing in its intensity, bringing louder and louder cracks of thunder with it.

I resolved to keep talking because I was afraid if I took a break she might decide it was time to finish me.

"You were careful not to touch the doorknob or the frame of the door, but you forgot that you touched the post of the porch cover. That's where the police found your fingerprint. It proves you had been to Todd's apartment. You were afraid, weren't you? Afraid that Todd may tell the police, or in this case, myself that you knew more about what was going on than you let on."

As unsettled as Andrea had been, she was now the picture of cold and calculated. I felt like I had to go on though, or she may finish me then turn on Tuttle. I was running out of clues. And she seemed to be running out of patience.

"Autumn must have found out about your... colorful... past. She was scared of you, wasn't she? I bet she was afraid to tell you she didn't want to be best buddies with you because she was afraid she'd end up like people who have told you no in the past. It terrified her she'd end up dead. Am I right?" I said.

Not sure why I said it, but I was just spewing word vomit now. The lump in my thought wasn't enough to stop it anymore.

Andrea laughed a loud laugh. I realized I might have been off a little on that point. She looked unhinged after that last bit. I'd finally backed myself into a spot I wished I hadn't. I stumbled backwards and fell to a seated position. Crap.

Andrea hoisted back the limb over her head, ready to swing down on me, ready to end me and my unending blathering. My mother always said my mouth would get me in trouble someday. I guess she was right.

Looking up at her as she looked back at me with a rage I've never been able to elicit in a woman without dating them, the lightning lit up the sky behind her, blinding me for a moment. The thunder cracking almost instantly, loudly and seeming to take even Andrea by surprise as I could audibly hear her gasp, even if I couldn't see her yet.

Then I heard and felt the thunder roll. As my eyes readjusted to my surroundings I saw Andrea, still looming over me, but her arms were hanging loosely at her sides, the limb laying on the ground at her feet. She was still looking me in the eye, but her focus seemed to be through me, not on me.

As my eyes adjusted to the darkened night sky even more, I saw it. The blood was wicking all over the front of her shirt and down her pants.

Then she collapsed.

A couple of yards away I saw the smoking, and shaking, gun. Holding it was Autumn.

Even the driving rain couldn't hide the tears streaming down her face. She looked broken and terrified. Then she dropped the gun and collapsed to her knees, sobbing and screaming.

I looked to see Tuttle, on his feet finally, nursing a broken hand and possibly forearm. The police sirens and lights were approaching. It had seemed like an eternity, but apparently it had all happened very quickly. Strange how something so terrifying can see like it lasts forever when, in reality, it was fleeting.

Then I felt the fight or flight finish its run. I suddenly felt like I could sleep for days. I fell back in the grass and took a breather as the uniformed officers took Autumn into custody and the EMTs rushed to check on Tuttle and Andrea.

CHAPTER FORTY-FOUR

AUTUMN BAYLOR COLLAPSED. She was sobbing on the ground only yards from the instrument that started this total fiasco.

The officers were on scene now in full force. She was being taken into custody for killing Andrea Keller.

"You should also add for the murder of Brenda Clark." I said.

Autumn didn't look at me or say anything immediately, but her body language said it all. I was right. She looked even more broken than she had a moment ago. Then she simply said, "It was all too much."

"Andrea was protecting you, wasn't she?" I asked. "All the rude comments, all the blocking... she was trying to keep us off your trail. She may have said nothing, but she became obsessed with you. Just like her friend in high school. The one she attacked when she betrayed her trust. You found out about that and, not that you were afraid to push her away, but instead, you turned it to your advantage and used Andrea as your own guard dog. I thought you were afraid of Andrea, but you were afraid of people finding out you killed Clark. Andrea wasn't hovering over you against your will, you had her protecting you!"

Tuttle was letting the paramedic wrap his hand. He winced, but still had to ask Autumn, "What happened that night... the night Clark was killed?"

Autumn had stopped crying out loud by now, and she seemed more in a trance than anything else. She just stared at the Bösendorfer and where Andrea Keller's body still laid.

"Andrea had stolen the piano for me... for me..." she said wistfully. "She knew I loved the piano. I told her I wanted it for myself. She had taken me to the warehouse and showed me what she'd done. Showed me the piano. Then she went out. She went out to get... champagne..." Autumn let out a little laugh. "I don't know, I guess to celebrate or something." She said. "I had no idea that was what she was doing. She was crazy. I wasn't going to celebrate with her. I had no idea she was even... doing that."

She looked thoughtful for a moment, then continued.

"I have to admit, once I saw it, and knew I had it, I wanted to keep it. I thought maybe..." she said, her eyebrows cocked like someone who wasn't looking to buy a guitar, but they just found a fantastic deal at my store.

I was seeing that Autumn was not the innocent girl everyone thought she was. She seemed less upset that she killed Clark, or even Keller, but more upset that the whole thing was falling apart. She had used Andrea's friendship and devotion to her to manipulate her into eliminating anyone who would have come close to the secret she was trying to cover up.

"While Andrea was out of the warehouse, I'm assuming that Clark arrived, having tracked down the moving company herself because she could be a little more influential in getting information from the movers. By that I mean, she was scary." I said.

I turned to Tuttle and I'm sure my eyes must have looked wild, because everything made sense now.

"When Clark showed up at that warehouse and found Autumn with the piano, she assumed Autumn had stolen it. I bet she started ranting at Autumn and maybe even became violent." I said.

"Autumn, you broke the lid prop off and defended yourself by swinging at Clark's head, hitting her and knocking her towards the piano. Remember what Raines said about the blow to the head?" I said, pointing at Tuttle like I dared him to recall. "Clark's head struck the piano, and the combined head trauma killed her!" I might actually have sounded excited now. "When Andrea returned to the scene, she dropped the champagne in panic and she and Autumn both hoisted Clark up and into the piano in a rush and ran."

I had to take Autumn's silence as confirmation.

"Take her in. I'll be there after I get cleared by medical." Tuttle said, nodding to the officer that had Autumn in cuffs now.

"You have the right to remain silent…" the officer started with her Miranda rights. She just looked at the ground as the officers led her toward the squad car.

"How's the hand, Mark?" I asked Tuttle, who was looking as tired as I felt.

"Yeah, it hurts like heck, but I'll be okay."

I thought about Sarah and Trevor, and realized how close I had come to not seeing them again. I was given a chance to see the people I loved again. I wasn't sure I was ready to use the L-word for Sarah just yet, but I was certainly glad I was going to get the chance to see where things led.

"Me too, buddy. Me, too." And I knew I was going to be okay.

I pulled out my phone and dialed Sarah's number as I stepped away from all the hullaballoo to get a little privacy, though I wasn't at all sure I even cared who heard what I was about to say.

"Hey, Jack! What's up?" Sarah said, sounding chipper. She obviously hadn't continued listening to the police band radio this evening, and didn't know what had just happened.

"Hey, Sarah. I just wanted to call you and say that I have been thinking about us, and you, and… well, I want to know if you'd like to give us a chance? You and me. Together?"

I took a deep breath and waited. I was nervous, but I knew this was something I wanted, and I had to know now if it was something Sarah wanted, too.

"Well, Jack. If I didn't want to give it a shot, I wouldn't have said I'd have dinner with you to begin with. Of course I want to give us a chance!" she said.

I laughed in spite of myself! I couldn't hold it back, the happiness. I felt my heart open up again. It had been like they had buried my heart with Michelle, but now I felt it beating again, and quickly, at that!

"I'm so happy to hear you say it! I was gonna burst!" I said, sounding like a teenager in love.

Maybe I was. Not a teenager. In love.

I didn't know for sure, but it sure felt that way! I knew I needed more time, and a certain level of infatuation was at play, especially at this stage of the relationship, but Sarah had opened something up in me, and I was glad to feel it. I needed it. I needed to move forward in life.

And now I just might have someone to move forward with me.

And maybe a few new friends, too.

Tuttle came over and gestured towards me. "The hands all good. Just a lot of swelling." He said as he held up a hand wrapped tightly in white gauze.

"Sarah, I'll be over soon. I've got a lot to tell you about my day." I said and hung up the phone.

Tuttle and I walked together in silence toward his old Caddie.

"Mark? Can you drop me off at Sarah's?" I asked.

He shot me a look like I was doing something sly. "You still have energy to go to Sarah's?" He asked.

"I'm pretty sure I can handle anything after today." I replied. "Besides, I could use a wonderful woman to come home to. I haven't been ready till now, but life has recently put a lot of stuff in perspective for me."

"I suppose so." Tuttle said. "I suppose so."

"Uh, Mark? I was meaning to ask you…" I trailed off for a moment as we started walking towards Tuttle's old Caddie.

"What is it?"

"So, I'd been thinking about taking classes to become a private investigator." I waited for Tuttle to laugh. He didn't.

"You've got a knack for this stuff, I admit, but why give up your true love?" He said. "Music is what drives you."

I knew he was right. Just the thought of not running my music store made me feel weird.

"Well, you know me pretty well! Anyway, I just hired a new employee who needs to learn the ropes. Who knows? She may take over the business one day! So, you don't mind me helping you out on your really juicy cases, do you?" I asked.

Tuttle just shook his head and pinched the bridge of his nose.

"Could I stop you from giving your input, even if I didn't want it?"

"So glad to hear that, Mark! I'd love to help!" I said.

Tuttle stopped in his tracks, and honestly, looked a little shell-shocked.

"Uh, well…. I guess we'll figure it out." he said. And I was relieved. It's always good when you can learn from a brilliant detective and a great friend.

Speaking of great friends, or maybe more, I needed to get to Sarah's.

"Let's get me to one Sarah Laney's!" I shouted.

"Calm down, Casanova. I'm nursing a bum hand here." Tuttle said.

"Well, put some ice on that thing and let's get going. Or maybe I should call Raines? She likes me and she can drive, right?"

"Don't bring her into this."

"Okay, but she likes me best."

Tuttle looked amused.

"Keep telling yourself that, Jack."

"I will. And that reminds me, I need to stop for some coffee on the way."

"Good lord, Jack. More coffee? After today, you need a man's treat. How about we grab a cheeseburger?."

"Never!" I exclaimed, but thought about it for a moment.

"Well, maybe a quick one."

Made in the USA
Columbia, SC
25 September 2024